A strange and wondrous animal . . .

In her family's tipi Kit Fox was nothing special to anyone. Not a son. Not beautiful. Only a middle child. But to the horse she was special. This morning he had let her touch him. No one else in the band had done that without harm. Almost none of her people, the Blood tribe, had ever seen a horse before, and the people were shy of this strange animal.

Kit Fox knew better. She thought of her awe at this new and wondrous animal, her joy in watching his powerful stride over the prairie. And more than anything else in the world she wanted to ride him. To fly with him, like an eagle, over the hills to the fork of the rivers. She knew that she could learn to ride, if only the others would let her.

◆——◆◼◆◼◆——◆

"The plot is fast-paced and believable. The time and place are well established, and the characters, multi-dimensional."
—*The Horn Book*

OTHER PUFFIN BOOKS YOU MAY ENJOY

Jan Hudson
DAWN RIDER

PUFFIN BOOKS

AUTHOR'S NOTE

My thanks to the following: Susan Grattan, Art and Sue Lamothe, Marie Wiedrick, Pearl Wahlberg, Jan Cormeau and Delia Wiedrick. For commentary on the manuscript itself, I thank: Jennifer Nyhof, Bill Godfrey and his classes at Malmo Elementary, Cora Taylor, the children of Joussard School, Jan Truss and Beverly Hungry Wolf. A special thanks is due my editor, Paula Wiseman.

PUFFIN BOOKS
Published by the Penguin Group
Penguin Putnam Books for Young Readers,
345 Hudson Street, New York, New York 10014, U.S.A.
Penguin Books Ltd, 27 Wrights Lane, London W8 5TZ, England
Penguin Books Australia Ltd, Ringwood, Victoria, Australia
Penguin Books Canada Ltd, 10 Alcorn Avenue, Toronto, Ontario, Canada M4V 3B2
Penguin Books (N.Z.) Ltd, 182-190 Wairau Road, Auckland 10, New Zealand

Penguin Books Ltd, Registered Offices: Harmondsworth, Middlesex, England

First published in the United States of America by Philomel Books,
a division of The Putnam & Grosset Book Group, 1990
Published by Puffin Books,
a member of Penguin Putnam Books for Young Readers, 2000

10 9 8 7 6 5 4 3 2 1

THE LIBRARY OF CONGRESS HAS CATALOGED THE PHILOMEL EDITION AS FOLLOWS:
Hudson, Jan, 1954–1990 Dawn rider / by Jan Hudson.
p. cm.
Summary: Kit Fox's sixteenth year with her people, the Bloods, is filled with
preparations for an important buffalo run, talk of her older sister's coming
marriage, and skirmishes with their traditional enemy the Snakes.
ISBN 0-399-22178-6
1. Sihasapa Indians—Juvenile Fiction. [1. Sihasapa Indians—Fiction.
2. Indians of North America—Great Plains—Fiction.] I. Title.
PZ7.H8665Daw 1990 [Fic]—dc20 89-29557 CIP AC

ISBN 0-698-11859-6

Printed in the United States of America

The people in this story are not historical personages,
but fictional creations. The events, however, are based on
written records of the Blackfoot Nation of 1730–1740.
The Blackfoot tribes occupied portions of what is now
northern Montana and Alberta, Saskatchewan.

DAWN RIDER

CHAPTER ONE

With part of her mind she heard Found Arrow's voice. "Careful, careful, Kit Fox. I am trying to hold him steady, but I do not know what he is going to do!"

Kit Fox thought, Why should I listen to him? Found Arrow does not understand my dream of riding the horse. His warnings are not real. She felt the horse's hair, still damp from the dew of the early spring morning. She heard the rustling sound of the horse's feet as they shifted in the meadow grasses. Those things were real.

Such a beautiful animal. She whispered his name. "Eagle Flies Over Hills. My horse, my wild, handsome horse." The smell of his sweat filled her nostrils. She thought how she wanted to run her hands over his high ears. They were strong like those of her own namesake, the Kit Fox.

In her family's tipi she was nothing special to anyone. Not a son. Not beautiful. Only a middle child. But to the horse she was special. This morning he had let her touch him. No one else in the band had done that without harm. Almost none of her people, the Blood tribe, had ever seen a horse before, and the people were shy of this strange animal.

Kit Fox knew better. She thought of her awe at this new and wondrous animal, her joy in watching his powerful stride over the prairie. How good it felt when she stroked the horse's long muzzle, soft as the fuzz on deer antlers in spring. He was so tall. The people had named him "ponokamita," a bearer of burdens like the dog, but tall as the elk. And more than anything else in the world she wanted to ride him. To fly with him, like an eagle, over the hills to the fork of the rivers. She knew she could learn to ride, if only the others would let her.

And if he would trust her.

Kit Fox laid her head against the horse's golden-brown coat and heard his quick breathing. A wise hunter had taught her that if she wanted to calm an animal there must be no smell of fear or anger on her. And Kit Fox knew the only way not to smell of these things was not to feel them.

They breathed together now, in one strong rhythm, the slow shushing sound of their breath stirring the early morning air like a breeze.

"Found Arrow," she whispered to her distant cousin, "hold the lead near the horse's mouth. I want to try to lie on him so he can feel all my weight on his back. Not to put my foot over—just to lie on him."

"Kit Fox, why try? He will only throw you. And if anyone sees you there will be trouble."

"I will not stay up there long. Please hold him steady."

She knew her cousin would help her. They had been friends for a long time.

Then she vaulted her weight up and over onto the horse's broad back. She landed with her chest against her arms, legs dangling. She was on the horse! Kit Fox was so ecstatic she could barely hear Found Arrow.

"Kit Fox," said Found Arrow, "get down before he decides to bounce you off onto the ground the way he did Wolf Eater."

"You are just afraid because none of our warriors have ridden him yet," she said softly, so as not to disturb the horse. Kit Fox knew that other tribes had horses now, and that their people rode them without harm. The war chief, Kills Bear with Knife, had said so, and this was his horse.

Chief Kills Bear with Knife said their cousin tribe the Peigans had owned two horses since last autumn. She knew Found Arrow had heard the tales.

"Chief Kills Bear with Knife said the Peigans ride their horses and use them instead of dogs to haul travois, do you remember?" she reminded Found Arrow. He was the guard the chief had set for the horse, and if Found Arrow did not allow it, Kit Fox could not learn to ride. But her true wish was that Found Arrow would leave her and the horse, allowing them time alone.

"Chief Kills Bear with Knife!" Found Arrow protested. "He urged at council that we set warriors to guard the horse at first so we can learn about him. And that was because of Wolf Eater. You may wish to forget, but this horse tossed Wolf Eater onto the ground, kicked him and broke his thighbone."

But Kit Fox felt sure the horse would not hurt her. He

was too grand, too beautiful. With her feet dangling a foot above the ground, she was filled with excitement as the creature shifted restlessly. Kit Fox imagined what changes horses would bring to her life. When the band moved she would not be limited to the few items her dog could haul or she could carry. How good to have Eagle Flies Over Hills's help on the long march to the spring campsite. He could carry her painting kit and the blue and red embroidered dress that always weighed so heavy on her back.

Just then Found Arrow looked up and shook his head. "You should leave the horse to the care of the warriors," he told her. His voice was low, but firm. "This is the first and last day that I will help you put yourself in such danger."

"But why?" Kit Fox continued so as to lengthen her time on the horse. The wild beauty.

"Too many people have been hurt already through the horses. Not just Wolf Eater. Remember the One Bull band."

Kit Fox winced. The One Bull band, their nearest neighbors, had been slaughtered by the Snake people a moon ago. Her favorite aunt and cousins had been sent to the Sand Hills. Round prints had dappled the soft earth between bloody corpses and burned tipis, from one end of the camp ring to the other—the hoofprints of horses. The Bloods had heard that the Snakes had many of these new marvels, these horses. Now the enemy could strike this far north, into the plains on either side of the Red Deer River valley. Now that it was spring again, the marshes and the sloughs of melted snow would dry. Then the war parties would travel.

If only their people had horses, too, argued some of the younger band members. With the height and swiftness of the horse beneath them, Blood warriors would have equal power.

Kit Fox knew that her people must have horses, but she also heard the elders' warning that once the horse became part of the life of the Bloods, the tribe would change and change again.

She needed to convince Found Arrow. "I also mourn the fate of the One Bull band. Only horses can save us. And the First Maker sent me a dream in my sleep two nights ago, a vision of riding Eagle Flies Over Hills." The horse moved slightly beneath her.

Found Arrow shook his head, as if dismissing the possibility of sacred insights being sent to such a young woman.

"My grandmother has heard my dream," Kit Fox continued. "She tells me it was not an ordinary dream, but sacred and powerful. Will you not listen to the wisdom of Old Holy Woman? I have asked her in humility. I accept the vision as a holy burden, not as an honor. Help me."

"Why do you ask my help?"

"Do you not know? If you do not help me learn to ride the horse, I cannot follow my vision. I cannot do what the Creator has told me to do for our people." Hesitantly, she offered one more reason, keeping her voice as soft as she could to calm the horse. "And I will help you with your vision quest."

"You? How?" asked Found Arrow. He grinned.

"I could use what my father taught me to help you trap

the golden eagle with your hands, for feathers for your war shield."

"Did your brothers tell you it is my time for that? Then they have also told you that the old men will instruct me." Found Arrow halted. He twisted the lead in his hands.

Kit Fox repeated, "Please help. I must learn to ride." Still she spoke softly so as not to disturb the beast.

"Ride? You are dangling, not riding!" Found Arrow laughed. "You look as silly as a little girl with her legs tied around a dog's belly." His eyes gleamed black.

He will not hear me, Kit Fox thought. "Do you dare to tie me on him?" she taunted.

"Can you stay on by yourself?" A track like a crowsfoot sprang up between Found Arrow's eyebrows. "You are a girl, and he has already hurt a warrior. Even with everything the healer woman can do for Wolf Eater, she cannot be sure that his leg will heal straight. How can you, a girl—"

"Sixteen winters old," Kit Fox interrupted. She felt her body stiffen with tension. I must not forget my balance on the horse, she reminded herself.

Found Arrow repeated, "A girl. This matter of the new animal, this is a matter only for warriors."

"Just because no warrior has ridden the horse, why should I not try?" She knew that no one could understand the animal as she did.

"You are a girl. This is not a matter for women."

You sound like a boy, even if you are eighteen winters old, thought Kit Fox. But she did not want to offend him. She needed his help. "The dogs belong to the women," she reminded him. "Why would horses not also be a matter for women? And I am good with animals." The horse moved slowly forward as Kit Fox balanced herself on top.

"All animals adore you," agreed Found Arrow.

"No one will blame you if something happens," Kit Fox said. "You were guarding him, as you were supposed to do."

"I am not supposed to let people climb up on him."

"Did anyone say the horse could not be ridden? At council they agreed to keep him at the river meadow beyond the grove where we gather firewood. You are guarding him from the children. You are doing just what the elders decided."

Found Arrow's voice rose. "Kit Fox, do you not care that the beast is dangerous?"

She searched for an end to the quarrel. "Wolf Eater did not have you to hold the horse steady," she said. After a moment's silence on both parts, she added, "If you want to lead him forward slowly, I will be brave. Courage, my beauty," she murmured to the animal, as Found Arrow tugged on the reins and the horse paced forward.

Her body swayed. Her face rested against the warm, sweaty horse hair. She felt Eagle Flies Over Hills trembling. She and the horse moved together.

Suddenly the crack of an ax thundered from the forest. Quick as a rattlesnake, the horse's back arched, and Kit Fox flew up into the air. Her stomach wrenched. The horse squealed beneath her.

As she fell she grabbed for mane or ear or anything at

all to hold her. But the beast skittered from under her arms. She hit the dirt with the taste of fear in her mouth.

"You did not hold him!" Kit Fox croaked.

"Kit Fox, how could I see what he meant to do? Are you hurt?" asked Found Arrow. He noted, "Your eyes are bloodshot." Kit Fox did not try to answer.

Every bone in her body ached. She wished for her sister or mother to hold her in comforting arms.

She lay gathering her strength and watched Found Arrow gentling the horse. He offered it his hand for inspection. First, Eagle Flies Over Hills jerked his long nose back, his nostrils quivering. But Found Arrow held still until finally the horse nuzzled him.

"You did not hold him," Kit Fox repeated.

"Kit Fox, how was I to know what to do? What do I know about the ways of horses? But now I know the signs," Found Arrow told her. "His ears went back to his head. Then he bucked. I had to struggle just to hold onto the lead. He is a strong animal."

For a moment Found Arrow stared at something over Kit Fox's head. Then he said, slowly, as if the words had to be forced out over some great reluctance, "You know you are my good friend, but, Kit Fox, why do you not wait until we have the chance to take counsel from the Peigans? They know so much already that you could not learn alone without pain."

Seeing that the light had shifted from early dawn to the brightness of true morning, Kit Fox chose not to argue. Soon the whole camp would be waking. She must return. "You are right, my friend. But the horse is special to me—the Creator has sent the vision to tell me so. Somehow, I must ride him."

She raised her sore body from the grass. There was a big smudge now on her workdress skirt. She hit at it with her palm. She pulled the leather down over her leggings from where the skirt had scrunched at her thighs.

"Your being here is a problem," Found Arrow said at last. "If the other children see you they will want to play with the horse, too." The early morning light traced the worrylines pressed between his brows.

She snorted. "You know that only the women are up at this time, to haul the water and start the fires. And a few hunters. The children—and almost all the men—are still asleep."

Found Arrow sighed. A light breeze stirred the cottonwoods shading the placid waters of the Red Deer River, as Kit Fox joined him beside the horse. For a few quiet moments they groomed the animal from opposite sides.

Kit Fox watched Found Arrow's hands move on Eagle Flies Over Hills. "You love the horse as much as I do. I see it. You want to see him run, too, like an eagle flies, over the hills."

"It is a good name," Found Arrow said, with a small smile. "Eagle Flies Over Hills."

Kit Fox smiled back. The wind blew in gusts now, rocking the crow's nest that hung above them. Straggly as a madman's hair it teetered between the poplar's forked branches. Despite her lingering pain, she looked forward to riding the horse again tomorrow.

Kit Fox never noticed the newcomer jogging down the

17

trail's little rise, coming from the downriver direction of the wood and the camp, until his heavy footsteps sounded like thunder in her ears. It was Raven Tail Feathers, Found Arrow's older half-brother. She wondered what he would think of her visiting Found Arrow without a chaperone. She probably should explain she had only come to look at the horse, so Raven would not discover her plan. She bit her lips, and decided on silence for now.

Kit Fox stared up at Raven Tail Feathers' face. Surely, he was one of the handsomest men among all the Blackfoot, and Kit Fox's older sister liked him very well. Too, too well. Kit Fox had never been sure why she did not like him.

Raven Tail Feathers raised an eyebrow. "This one is nearly as pretty as her sister," he offered—a great compliment, she knew.

Only last night a young man had sung and played the flute outside their family's tipi, from sunset to gray dawn. Kit Fox thought it had been Raven. Even with his buffalo robe pulled over his head, she could tell from the man's height. She wished desperately that it might have been someone else. After all, stories of Many Deer's beauty had spread far and wide. Everyone knew she was a fine cook, good with thread and awl, and quick to laugh. Many must desire her, Kit Fox thought, comforting herself. Raven Tail Feathers had not yet caught her.

If it had been him by the tipi, he had a haunting voice for singing love songs. Kit Fox had guessed without seeing that her sister smiled in the darkness. Someday, maybe, Kit Fox hoped, a young man would sing and play the flute that way for her.

The brothers greeted each other. "Did you come to the river to see Kit Fox or the horse or me?" asked Found Arrow.

"Do I not see too much of you without ever having to look for you?" Raven Tail Feathers pushed Found Arrow's shoulder with enough affection to rock him.

"You promised to tell me today how you trapped the eagles with your hands. I need to learn how, brother."

"Maybe tonight. You are going to do it?" Raven Tail Feathers asked.

"For feathers for my shield." Found Arrow drew himself up straight, as he continued to groom the horse.

Now his brother answered more seriously. "That is the right way—then the feathers will have power. But you will need to hear the stories of several men. How many warriors have you asked?"

"Kills Bear with Knife, Black Badger, Three Young Calves and you. I think I will also ask Kit Fox to tell me all her father taught her about eagles."

Kit Fox flushed. Would Raven respect the opinion of any woman?

Raven glanced at her. "It is not wrong to ask everyone."

Suddenly he shook himself, like a bear coming out of the water. He snatched the lead from Found Arrow's hand and roared, "Stand back!" as the others jumped to get away. He jerked, and the horse swung into a trot.

Eagle Flies Over Hills circled the warrior's body at the

length of his lead, struggling to escape. The whites of his eyes gleamed in terror. Foam sprayed from his lips.

"Do you see how quickly this animal learns from me?" Raven yelled.

Kit Fox held one hand over her heart. She had been sure that they were going to be trampled.

"See this horse!" Raven Tail Feathers shouted. "I will haul him around as I have hauled the great white-headed eagle. I will train him as I would train a dog or a woman! I will crack his head on a rock! I will make a necklace of his teeth if he does not obey me! Hi-yah!"

CHAPTER TWO

Kit Fox leaned toward Found Arrow and whispered, "I will not watch. The horse should not be treated this way."

"You are leaving?"

"My mother and grandmothers always expect me to be in camp to help them, once the sun has risen and the dawn hunting time is over. Will you be on guard again tomorrow?"

"Yes. Chief Kills Bear with Knife may guard with me, though," Found Arrow said. "If you come, you should bring a chaperone."

Kit Fox chewed her lip.

"Maybe your sister?" he added.

"Maybe my beautiful sister?" She had trouble hearing him with Raven Tail Feathers whooping at the horse so near them. Found Arrow thought of her, Kit Fox, only as a child. "No one in my family notices what I do or wonders where I have gone. No one will miss me and if they do, they will guess I am hunting some small creatures for our stew pot."

"Well, come just one more morning, then," Found Arrow said.

Camp lay in the direction of the risen sun. As Kit Fox came over a rise she noticed the cloven hoofprints dappling the gray earth before her. A deer must have walked there in earliest morning, when the ground was still moist from the rain at nightfall. Now the clay had dried and the lips of the prints cracked like ill-made pots. I wish I had waited here for her, thought Kit Fox. Here in sight of the huddled gray shades of the tipis. I would have asked her forgiveness, and drawn my arrow, delicate as the bone of a deer's leg, swift as a deer in motion. Then my family would have good food to eat—food that I brought them.

She ducked through the tipi flap and five heads turned to greet her. She nodded to both her grandfather's co-wives, her parents and her older sister. The latest baby slept in his mossbag. Kit Fox smiled as she breathed the smells of buckskin, wood smoke and warmth that meant home and family. The others smiled back at her, then returned to their conversation.

Kit Fox marked a place for herself on one of the soft, furry, hide-covered sleeping couches that ringed the back of the tipi. Before she sat, she filled a bowl full to the brim with berry soup from the hearth in the center. Then she knelt quietly between her older sister and her grandmother, Old Holy Woman. When a chance came, Kit Fox leaned close to her sister and whispered into her ear. "I spoke with Raven Tail Feathers this morning. He was with Found Arrow."

"I thought you had gone out early to hunt." Many Deer had not turned her head, but at least she was smiling.

Kit Fox swallowed a wet ball at the back of her throat and explained, bravely, "I saw the horse. Found Arrow was guarding him."

Her sister's lashes flickered against her cheek. "How did Raven Tail Feathers look?"

Kit Fox sucked in her lip. So Many Deer had no concern about her younger sister visiting a man or about the horse. She only cared to hear about Raven Tail Feathers.

"He looked, oh, like the hero of a legend, very fine," Kit Fox admitted. At her sister's expectant silence, she continued, "You know. He had his hair pulled back in three parts," and she gathered her own locks in her hands to show how. "It was tied with hawkfeathers and shells and buckskin laces."

"Ahh."

"Many Deer, was that Raven outside our tipi last evening?" Kit Fox whispered. The others were talking loudly now about the war chief's recent vision of battle with the Flathead tribe.

"Yes. I think so. Did he look sleepy when you saw him this morning?" asked Many Deer.

"No."

"What moccasins was he wearing? Were they embroidered?" Many Deer smiled eagerly.

"Why? You did not embroider a pair of moccasins for him, did you?" Kit Fox's heart was a frozen stone. She knew what this would mean to any girl of the Bloods or any other of the Blackfoot tribes.

23

"No . . . not yet. Do you not think that I would have told my sister if I was to be married?"

"Maybe," said Kit Fox. The berry soup tasted good. Many Deer must have cooked it, or perhaps their grand-father's second wife, Swift Hands Woman. Their father's voice boomed in the background, telling a tale of one of his war visions, and the great victory he found when he followed it. None of the adults would turn an ear to the girls' conversation. Kit Fox crushed a saskatoon berry between her teeth for the sake of its sweet flavor. "And to answer your question, yes, Raven's moccasins were decorated with a red and white crooked-nose pattern. Did some other unmarried woman make them?"

"Kit Fox, you are a tease. I wonder if I should sew him moccasins with a red and white pattern, also. Could you ask Found Arrow if those are the colors that Raven likes? Found Arrow should know; he is Raven's brother." Many Deer did not pause to look at her younger sister. "Or perhaps I should sew moccasins in different colors, but in the same pattern? What do you— Kit Fox—!"

Bowl and spoon dropped from Kit Fox's hands, and berry soup sprayed across their laps. Drops of purple sank into their skirts.

"I am sorry, Many Deer," she mumbled.

Both of them were aware that their elders were pretending not to notice. Kit Fox plucked damp berries from the couch the girls shared, dropping them back into her bowl, one by one. "Many Deer, are you certain you want to marry Raven?"

"Why?" The word was toneless, revealing no emotion. Both girls kept their voices low.

"I . . . I . . ." More than anything, Kit Fox did not want to hurt her sister, but she felt she had to be truthful. "He is very handsome, very brave but . . . somehow . . . I cannot admire Raven." She thought of how Raven had threatened to make the horse's teeth into jewelry. Slowly she told the tale to her sister.

Old Holy Woman, their grandmother, spoke up now, as if she felt she had been overlistening long enough. "Ee-hee-hee-hee! Hear this, all of you. Our Kit Fox does not wish her sister to marry Raven Pinfeathers!"

"Raven Tail Feathers, Grandmother!" protested Many Deer.

"Tail Feathers, Pinfeathers," the old lady was nudging her co-wife to join in laughter. She pincered the roll of fat around her waist between thumbs and index fingers and joggled it, her remaining fingers spread over the mound of her belly as it heaved in time to her giggles. "Pinfeathers, the handsome fellow!"

"Has my mother heard rightly?" Whiteweasel's voice was good-natured as ever, but Kit Fox knew that for once she—not her brothers, not her beautiful sister—had her father's full attention.

She whispered, "Raven said he would make the horse's teeth into jewelry if the horse did not obey him."

"Any true woman or man would rather die than obey after such a threat," her father observed, "but are horses not more like dogs than like people?"

For a moment Kit Fox held her tongue while she wound her courage into a throwing-ball. She looked at

25

her father's chin, not at his eyes, while she lobbed the question with gentle courtesy. She knew that he preferred her brave, but always careful of a Blackfoot child's right manners. "It may be so. You know better than I, Father. But Raven also said he would train the horse in the same way he would train a dog—or a woman."

"Hear her," said skinny old Swift Hands Woman, nodding her head slowly.

"There is something to hear in what you say," agreed Whiteweasel. "But remember, Raven Tail Feathers is a man. He is accustomed to such ways of seeing things. He is, after all, a brave warrior, a fine hunter, of good family. He also," with a little smile for the pretty Many Deer, "gives much pleasure to look at. He will be a great man, likely a war chief—"

"Yes," breathed Many Deer.

"—and if he shows judgment and generosity, maybe a band chief. He is a good man, but he does not see the world as you do.

"Also, do not forget that such a man's first wife, his sits-beside-him wife, has many duties, and it would be comforting to her to have her younger sister beside her, in her tipi."

Kit Fox clamped her hand hard over her mouth and bit on the middle finger. Dimly she was aware of Old Holy Woman's arm around her from one side, and Many Deer's comforting pressure against the other.

Her father continued, "Think well about this, Kit Fox. Your mother and I had hoped that, since you girls are so close to each other—"

Whiteweasel's voice was interrupted by the face of Kit Fox's oldest brother, grinning through the tipi flap. Powerful medicine herb scents relaxed everyone and provided an end to her father's probing—for the moment.

Kit Fox guessed Antelope Runner had rubbed scented grease over his entire body, from his hair to his toes and fingers. There would be a ceremonial purpose to that, she knew, but since it would be a purpose of one of the men's secret societies, she did not know what. Antelope Runner's long and luxuriant hair, black as a raven's wing, was drawn tightly to cover his ears.

Bad Eyes, her second brother, followed Antelope Runner into the tipi. Like his elder, he wore only leggings with no shirt above them, but he carried a cougar-skin quiver, from which the paws of the cougar dangled. Bad Eyes, too, grinned from ear to ear as the young men greeted their father.

"Sons," said Whiteweasel. He waved a hand for them to sit. Not until each had a bowl of the berry soup was their news asked of them.

It was good news, enough to remove every other thought for the moment. Chief Kills Bear with Knife had announced the scouts had found a large herd of buffalo near the drive lines for the buffalo jump. The band could probably chase the herd between the lines and over the cliff, and capture them. Kills Bear asked all who could to help the huntmaster repair the buffalo jump. The corral, or piskan, under the cliff must be mended. The piles of stones that outlined the drive lines, out across the prairie as far as the eye could see, these must be built up again. Their tips could be extended with piles of brush or bones or dried dung. "And the runner," the sisters begged. Kit Fox could not control her giggle. "Who has been asked to be the buffalo runner?"

"Yes, tell us, what brave man is to be the decoy who leads the buffalo to us?" Old Holy Woman asked, her cheeks pink with such a glow that she could not disguise it. She and Swift Hands Woman touched elbows and smiled at each other.

"The one who is to lead the buffalo," Bad Eyes smiled at his modest brother, "though he will not tell you, is Antelope Runner."

Kit Fox watched her father's face fill with pride. He stood and reached across the hearth to his oldest son. Then the women congratulated Antelope Runner, each in turn.

As if he could hold himself back no longer, Antelope Runner threw down spoon and bowl, shot to his feet and declared, "I will lead the buffalo to my people—I will, if the spirits will aid me. I will pull over my head the horns and the robe of the calf that we shot today—" He gestured with hands over his head, curved into buffalo horns, acting out the hunt. He slunk toward his mother. "I will creep up to the edge of the herd from windward, then away, then toward them, as if I were a frightened orphan, until one of the cows worries for me and follows."

His mother nodded her head as if to say that she would gladly follow him, if she were a cow buffalo.

"Then a buffalo will follow the cow, then three, then a dozen, toward the hill that leads up to the cliff above the piskan. Now I am between the drive lines. The herd is behind, though they are not walking the trail one behind the other now. They are trotting neck and neck and now they are running!" He ran around the tipi fire staring over his shoulder as if something pursued him. Everyone pulled their legs back so he could pass before them.

Bad Eyes clapped out a drumbeat to make the sound of the hooves following: Tarrat, tarrat, tarrat, tarrat!

"Now I must run—fast—faster. The buffalo must become a river behind me, a fast river, a river with rapids. Any who hesitate will be crushed beneath a thousand hooves!"

Bad Eyes accelerated the beat. Tarrat, tarrat, tarrat . . .

Antelope Runner continued. "Though I run so fast I think I am the Wind himself, soon they will overtake me and I will be ground to dust beneath their feet. The hill looms ahead of me, and behind the high piles of boulders I glimpse my people, yelling and screaming to scare the stampede on. All the while the buffalo thunder at my heels. It is too late for them to turn back. We are coming over the final rise. Now the cliff will open under our feet." He panted, his hand pressing at his gut to show his exhaustion. "Now I fling off the calf robe from my shoulders. With the weight of the hundreds thundering behind them, the lead buffalo cannot slow at the sight of man. The drive lines close as we race toward the cliff edge—

"My people are screaming, they wave their arms at me. The ceremonies were done right, I have done right. The buffalo cannot escape us. I run near the boulders.

The people are jumping, and shaking their robes. The buffalo are afraid of them; I am only afraid of the buffalo. I jump the boulders, fall on my side as I slide over. A buffalo follows. But Bad Eyes—"

Antelope Runner dropped to the floor of the tipi and clutched his brother. The drum fell silent.

"Bad Eyes shoots him!"

Bad Eyes drew his bow back and loosed an imaginary arrow. The brothers flung their arms over their heads and cheered. Their audience grinned.

"That buffalo, it was really very close to me," Bad Eyes explained. "That's why I could see it."

Everyone laughed, and pounded them both on the shoulders. Even fragile Swift Hands Woman laughed hard.

Antelope Runner laid his head on his mother's lap. It was over. "I will not put my foot in a badger's hole when I run, Mother, will I, or trip over a rock?"

"Do not fear, my son. Too much fear is dangerous. The buffalo stones will aid you. Powerful ceremonies will aid you. Even I, your mother, will pray for you."

"Will you? And will my grandmothers and sisters also?"

The old women nodded. "I will seek a vision," promised Old Holy Woman.

"I will stay in the lodge and burn a braided rope of sweetgrass while I pray for you," Many Deer stated firmly.

"Kit Fox? Will you also pray?"

She loved her brother and wished him well. But she knew that she would rather be with her own bow and

30

arrows at the piskan, if she was permitted. She would ask Whiteweasel later, when he was alone. Now she said only, "Brother, I will help you however I can."

The men and the older women sat discussing at length the details of the ceremonies that must be followed, with Antelope Runner's buffalo stones and with those that were part of the sacred beaver medicine bundle. Kit Fox and Many Deer decided to walk upstream along the river leading to the buffalo corral to see if any of the berries were ripe enough for picking.

It was a long and silent walk. Only when they turned at the bend in the river and saw the piskan site, so far away that the figures of people moved over it like flies, did Kit Fox speak.

"I did not mean to worry you, Many Deer. I know you like that handsome man," she said bravely. Kit Fox did not know what was best to say. She loved her sister. But however gentle Kit Fox might be, she was also clear and firm and honest. She knew that if Many Deer asked her, she would have to say words her sister would not like, so she turned her head away.

Wind shuddered through the stunted willows on the sandbar. Long narrow leaves shook like boneless fingers as they blew. Behind the silvery green of the willows, Red Deer River flowed sluggishly. The sun had not yet made the berries ripe in their color, and none begged to be picked from the vine.

Many Deer spoke. "Look at the sky. It will rain before sunset. But the cloud is thin as a worn-out tipi cover. A light rain only, I would guess."

"I like the wind that comes before the rain," Kit Fox

agreed. "It blows the mosquitoes off before they have time to bite." She brushed Many Deer's wrist. "This weather has as much to be said for it as Raven Tail Feathers says for himself!"

Many Deer laughed softly. "Come with me!" she cried, and she pulled Kit Fox through a gap in the willows to a pebbled, sheltered shore. They perched themselves on a large boulder with a smooth, flat surface, well-warmed by the sun. Many Deer smiled and told her sister, "This is where I come to think or pray, and watch the river."

"It is good!"

"We are sisters, are we not? We share good things together?"

Kit Fox swallowed hard with the thought of where this trail of words seemed to be leading. "Usually we share good things, when we both like them."

"But you do not want to share my tipi with me, and our children, and our household?" her sister asked.

"Oh, Many Deer, not because of you! You are my best friend and I will be so lonely when you marry. But most Blackfoot women do not choose to have co-wives, and most families have only one man and one woman. And I would not wish the husband you are choosing." Now she was saying everything she felt. Finally.

But her sister was not answering.

"Many Deer," Kit Fox continued, her voice on the edge of a wail, "are you sure you want Raven? He is so handsome. Widows and others will always be under his nose, trying to get his attention. Do you really think he is a man who will resist their flattery?"

32

"No," admitted Many Deer, as the two made their way back to the trail.

Kit Fox stared at her. Many Deer added, speaking slowly, "But I am as beautiful as he is handsome. He will always be afraid that if he behaves too poorly I will leave him, and some other man will have me for his partner."

Kit Fox bit her lip.

Many Deer's voice pleaded for agreement. "And my parents and my brothers would never let a husband abuse me. Or you, Kit Fox!"

Kit Fox bit her cheek. She suspected Raven of wishing to hurt the creatures of the First Maker, whether they were horses or women. She feared for her sister. But what more could she say? For herself, she wanted a man who did not seek more than one woman. She wanted to be the one wife of her own husband.

"It is not that I do not like living with you, Many Deer," she said. "How I wish you would stay in our parents' tipi. We are so happy. Why does anything have to change?"

"Old Holy Woman and Swift Hands Woman are happy as co-wives." The older girl paused for a moment at the bend in the trail. In a few more steps they would be through the willows, and sighting down the river to the corral, the piskan.

"But, Many Deer, they wanted that—and did not have much choice either. So many of the young men of their band had been killed fighting the Assiniboin. You know that in such times many women have no choice except to be co-wives. Or how would they marry at all?"

"And now the warriors' talk is all of horses and thundersticks and other things for more war and more deaths. Bad times for women," Many Deer predicted.

"The horses will mean good times for women! We will ride over the prairie, free as the wind," Kit Fox assured her sister. She wished she dared say more. She tagged Many Deer's shoulder. "There is the buffalo jump! Race me there!"

CHAPTER THREE

They sprinted along the mud flats under the sandstone bank of Red Deer River. The river curled on the other side of their path, narrow and twisted as a garter snake. Under the sharpest cliff stood the buffalo piskan. Kit Fox ran until her sister caught up with her, and then they stood puffing and blowing, leaning together, straining their eyes to see who had already come to help repair the corral.

"Look! The huntmaster is standing on the top of the cliff." The figure seemed to shimmer in the clear, dry air. Kit Fox bounced with excitement. "And down by the ruins of the corral—is that Found Arrow?" Someone must have relieved him from guard duty, she thought.

"Took Two Lance is with him, and that scruffy runt, Sun Smokes!" The sisters hurried to join the other young people. Even squinting and craning their necks, they could barely catch the gestures of the older, spiritually powerful warrior in charge of the hunt, the sun shone so brightly behind him. He was sighting down the drop to see how far the broken walls of the piskan must be extended, to hold any buffalo who survived with necks unbroken. Now he gestured with his arms.

Found Arrow ran across the river flat and halted at a wave from the huntmaster. Many Deer jogged in the other direction. The huntmaster waved her to stop. Wind laced through her hair and the grass as she waited then, sunk to her ankles in the fresh shoots of vetch and wild white sweet pea.

Her position and Found Arrow's marked the edges to which the corral must be rebuilt. The huntmaster turned to make his way back around and down to the river flats. He disappeared from their sight, as invisible from the cliff for the moment as the cliff would be to the driven herd of buffalo—until they topped the rise.

"I will wait for the huntmaster," volunteered Found Arrow.

Many Deer upended a stone so her place would not be forgotten. She cried to Kit Fox and the other youngsters walking toward her with questioning looks, "Next, we need willow branches, to weave the piskan walls again!"

"Yes!" agreed one of the older boys. "We used willow branches last time. I remember."

Laughing and pushing, they raced back to the trees near the bend in the river. They all knew what to do. Between them, they could remember most of the corral-building tradition so work began quickly. Their memory of tribal custom was all the direction that they needed.

"Willow, willow, willow—willow tea for Many Deer," sang Took Two Lance, in her sharp, high-pitched voice, as she swung a silver willow bough high over all their heads.

"Are you fevered, Many Deer?" another asked. "Do your joints ache, do your knees tremble with love for your sweetheart? Should we make you good medicine?"

Kit Fox answered them firmly. "She does not need your willowbark medicine." But Many Deer ignored them, working furiously instead among the willow bushes, ripping off springy branches longer than her friends' arms. Torn bits were thrown carelessly to crash behind her.

"Stop that! You will gouge out someone's eye if you are not more careful," Took Two Lance protested.

But Many Deer behaved as if she heard no one. Her back to them all, she hauled at a branch, thick as a lodgepole, until it snapped through its core. Fiercely she jerked and twisted the strip of connecting wood. It ripped away, leaving an ugly gash down the tree trunk.

"Many Deer is not the only one of us who has a man she likes." Kit Fox turned to Took Two Lance. I had better make a joke of this, she thought. She has no right to treat my sister so cruelly.

"I hear soon someone will stand by your tipi for you, Took Two Lance!" Kit Fox wrapped her cape to muffle her head and shoulders.

By sucking her cheeks in and shaping her mouth into a circle, she made her voice hollow and high as a ghost's. "Hear me, my name is Gorgeous Bald Eagle. I have walked across the broad waters and the mountains and the plains for love of your fair daughter and because

I hear she cooks such good berry soup. In my own country I was a war chief, I had much hair and I was fat."

"Kit Fox—" Took Two Lance groaned.

"But now I cannot eat or sleep because I so much like your fair daughter. I have walked so far to come to your tipi that I have grown thin and all my hair has fallen out. If you do not let me take her to my tipi where she can feed me berry soup, I may die."

Now all the others were laughing, even Many Deer. Took Two Lance countered, "Can it be Kit Fox you have come seeking? No, I cannot see how it could be her. If we let her feed you, you would surely never live."

Kit Fox decided to turn her back on this, deliberately directing her reply to the others in her audience. "No, it is not Kit Fox I seek, for her wisdom and beauty and skills do not extend to use of the cooking pot. No, I mean Took Two La—"

Kit Fox cocked her head, her spine stiffening at the buzz of a sparrow's alarm-trill behind her.

"What?—" She spun and crashed to the ground under the force of Took Two Lance's body.

Took Two Lance cried gleefully, "My name is Found Arrow. See how I have captured Kit Fox. I spend every morning with her by the river where I guard the strange horse creature—"

Kit Fox drove her free elbow into the other's ribs and went limp, signaling surrender. Took Two Lance stopped. There was no resistance.

All was silent except the rush of the river and the girls' panting.

Took Two Lance caught her breath to begin over in a deeper voice, "Hear me. As I told you, my name is Found Arrow. My brother Raven and I are under the love medicines of Whiteweasel's daughters. Though these two are not as talented or as pretty as many other girls of the band, we have eyes for no one except the beautiful Many Deer and her tagalong sister."

Kit Fox felt her whole body stiffen. "Jealous! Two Lance is jealous!" No one must suspect her plans to ride the horse or otherwise stop her from visiting him.

Their friends peered at them, and Sun Smokes smiled, lifting his hand so one dirty knuckle almost touched his mouth. Took Two Lance plunked her hips down firmly and reached for their sympathy with both hands. "Do you see how Kit Fox loses her temper when she is teased? How dare she say I am jealous!"

But Kit Fox did not reply with words. She lowered her head, arched her back and kicked out like a horse. Took Two Lance's front end shot forward, then down over the slope of Kit Fox's head as Kit Fox bucked. The onlookers gasped as the top of Took Two Lance's head hit the earth. But she rolled like a caterpillar to spread the impact along shoulders, hips, then thighs.

Forehead wrinkled, she pulled her skirt over her leggings with one angry hand. "Kit Fox! How did you do that kick?"

"I will show you," Kit Fox replied, and immediately the two were bucking with their heels on the grass. Kit Fox prayed the others would think the teasing about Found Arrow a joke like her own tale about Gorgeous Bald Eagle. Her secret was safe as long as none of them came down to the river in the early dawn hours to check and saw her with the horse.

The sun had risen a fingerwidth farther toward the height of the sky before long. Many Deer scolded them into taking up their stone knives and returning to the willows. "Lazy girls! Neither of you is worthy to be a Blackfoot woman!"

Kit Fox was just glad she and Took Two Lance were friends again. Good-enough friends. She grinned as she bundled branches energetically. The sun had hit the midpoint of the sky before everyone in their crew had all the weight they could carry. Laden, chatting, happy, the young people trudged back to the piskan.

On the ground by the ruins of the old enclosure was laid a row of logs, each as long as the height of a warrior. The huntmaster's crew of friends had cut these all in one morning and pointed their ends. Now they drove them into the resisting earth. Kit Fox, Sun Smokes and Many Deer laced the green shoots of willow in and out between the logs until they had a barrier that could hold back the charge of a maddened buffalo. The huntmaster had decided to add something not in the site's tradition.

"Do you see those stakes, sharpened at both ends?" Sun Smokes squealed. "Do you see how the warriors are wedging them so they stick out at an angle? Any buffalo who runs at the archers will smash on the stakes! He forces one of these into his chest—and he runs no more!"

"No buffalo are going to survive falling over the cliff," said Took Two Lance, and she smacked her fist on the stake Sun Smokes carried.

"And if they do survive, will the archers need to worry about them?" asked Kit Fox. She had already resolved to be among the archers. She was not too old for such games. "My father said that when the cliff is more than the length of ten buffalo falling head first one after the other, as this one is, a buffalo will break her legs when she lands. That is, if she does not fall on her head and kill herself."

"You speak truthfully," answered Sun Smokes, drawing his scrap of a body upright. "All the first buffalo over this cliff will die on landing. But did you notice the bone piles?"

His bright eyes surveyed their speechless faces. His voice fell modestly as he explained, "Chief Kills Bear with Knife explained this to me."

Under the talus slope at the base of the cliff, down the long walk to the cutting ground, the earth bore its bone piles. The band had not used this particular site for a number of years; in most places the sun-bleached bones were skinned over by the faint green of sage, by cactus, creeping juniper or the dead brown of dry rustling grasses. Dust blew between the spine lines of vertebrae.

Dust lay over the skulls like skin, and grass grew through their eye holes. On the flatter cutting ground toward the river, the greater moisture and soil had covered hundreds of corpses with prairie flowers. Foxtail barley curled under the strokes of wind as if some bones again grew fur. That was all Kit Fox had noticed. That there lay bones under the bones she also knew, and maybe bones under those, again. The buffalo jump had been used from time to time for many centuries. Maybe the bones at the bottom were rotten, or maybe they were hard as rock, like the stone-hard skeletons of giant animals found farther south in the badlands along this same river. Goose bumps rose on her arms.

"Look at them!" the boy said, his thin shoulders hunched intently. "Do you see how many of the skulls have lance marks or have been crushed in?"

This time Kit Fox protested. "That was to get the brains out, so the women can use them in tanning hides. We will have new buffalo skulls for that work, soon enough."

"Hear me!" Sun Smokes bent with his hand thrust in front of their eyes. With his other hand he grasped one of his fingers. "If the herd we drive is only a few buffalo, they come down over the cliff in this way—one crashes to the ground, another crashes to the ground, another crashes—and on the rocks they stagger or lie, all dead or almost dead. The archers will shoot any animal that moves."

Kit Fox nodded her head in agreement. Sun Smokes continued. "If the herd we drive is hundreds of buffalo, they come down like this—three crash to the ground, another five crash to the ground, another nine crash to the ground, and then they are coming steady as a waterfall—and at first they are all dead or almost dead. But it does not stop. Soon there are layers of buffalo. When one cow falls on four hooves, her legs maybe do not break against the stones. They sink into the side of some other cow. That body takes the weight of the fall for the live buffalo."

Took Two Lance gaped at him, suspicious. Sun

Smokes lifted his hands for her to see more closely. She tossed back her head and narrowed her eyes.

"The buffalo no longer fall like this," and Sun Smokes demonstrated by thumping his fist hard against his palm. "The buffalo fall on the bodies of their sisters and brothers in this manner. The bodies give; those who fall in the second wave almost bounce as they are landing. Many are alive—some have not been hurt at all."

He grabbed Took Two Lance's hand. "Let me show it on your palm."

"Ow!" yelped Took Two Lance.

When the work was done, Kit Fox dug in the drifted dust around the base of the talus slope under the cliff, looking for arrowheads. The sun was halfway down the sky. She had nineteen or twenty arrowheads before Found Arrow joined her.

"What are you collecting?" he asked, as she slid a palmed chip into her rawhide drawstring pouch.

She answered, "A gartersnake for Cub, among other things."

"What other things? Why are you still gathering arrowheads?"

A glint of a chalcedony point appeared under her moccasin. Her back to him, she crouched to pick it up. "Because you have not yet showed me how to make good ones." She wished Many Deer or one of the others would join them and interrupt his questioning. She did not need to explain what she was doing, nor did she want to.

"Women do not need to be good at such skills," replied Found Arrow. "And you know it."

"You know a good Blackfoot woman should be able to provide food for her family, in any time and any trouble. And I want to do better," said Kit Fox. "I still chip my points so they are too thick, or uneven, or not sharp enough."

"I have seen you shoot. You are more than good enough, for a woman."

"When we were children you said I was going to be one of the manly hearted women, with a man's powers and a man's skills as well as a woman's. Remember?"

"Yes, I do. That will come when you are older. Manly hearted women are usually older," Found Arrow replied.

What concern was this of his and what did he know about it, Kit Fox thought. He angered her, but when she studied his face, she had to admit to herself how much more attractive than his older brother she thought him.

She said, slowly, "You want to be a warrior, go through the ceremonies, seek power and make your war shield. That is something men usually do, for which I have no desire. But I also must fulfill the visions the Creator has sent me. I want to ride Eagle Flies Over Hills."

Found Arrow shifted on his feet.

Kit Fox opened her heart to him. "I love the horse— from the first time I saw him! He is our future. I even thought about him at the piskan. Can you imagine, if we drove the buffalo with horses? And I want to ride him, faster than a prairie fire—so beautiful and so powerful! Please, Found Arrow," begging, she gazed up at him, "will you help me?"

44

"Well," his voice rumbled, "you can come tomorrow morning. Then you can tell me the stories of how your father caught the eagles for his war shield feathers, and we will see."

She nodded. Silently, she prayed. Please, please, let him help me.

CHAPTER FOUR

Four walked downstream along the riverbank under the red sky of the next day's breaking dawn: Kit Fox, beside Found Arrow, beside Chief Kills Bear with Knife, beside Eagle Flies Over Hills. The horse was the only one who had to be there. He was tied to a long lead held in Kills Bear's hand, and he was sloshing knee-deep in water. Kills Bear had said this would make him more obedient.

"And I captured a fine new bow and Antelope Runner counted coup two times, touching the enemy," Kills Bear with Knife went on. He was telling a war story. Kit Fox felt lucky just to be permitted to be there, but then, Old Holy Woman had made that request of the war chief. She had told him that her granddaughter had a special interest in the chief's horse stories, as well as in his suggested methods for horse-breaking. So he did not question her being there.

"They killed young Star Dog then. He took an arrow

under his shoulder. But we killed three in that hunting party of the Kootenais. We knew we had to run. The survivors would bring all the men in their camp after us, they would be wanting to make the Blackfoot cry, wanting to kill us. I told the young men that every place we got water here, the Kootenais knew it, every war lodge or scout sight, every ravine we could hide in. It was their land. I was afraid.

"For two days we ate only dried meat. Made no fire. We did not want to signal where Blackfoot were camped. One time a grouse flew out of the brush, and I grabbed Raven's bow as he raised it. No shooting. No cooking. No fires. It was too dangerous.

"The third day we ran from gray dawn until it was almost too dark to see. We wanted to stay alive. That night we slept in a gully.

"The moon came out. The coyotes were singing. I am an experienced warrior, I listen to coyotes. Something was not right. I had dreamt that we were back in camp, and the camp was burning.

"I decided to crawl to the top of the gully. Now the moon was up, a moon small like the white at the base of a warrior's fingernail.

"Behind us, not too far, there shone a campfire. I thought of hot food. My stomach growled like a hungry bear. I woke the others. 'Our enemies are close behind us,' I said. 'We are hungry and cold, and they lie by their campfire. Do we run away by the moonlight—or do we make an ambush?'"

Found Arrow cleared his throat. "Was it a trap?"

Kills Bear with Knife laughed. "Did they guess we

might be that brave, that desperate? I chose Raven Tail Feathers and Antelope Runner, your brothers, as scouts to stalk the Kootenais with me. Anyone who came close to a guard was to give a sign—a night owl screech if it was me, a coyote yap if it was Raven, a great plains wolf howl if it was Antelope. Then we would know on which side of the fire the guard sat. If more than one of us cried out, we could still try our luck at getting away by moonlight.

"From what we had seen in the daytime I knew that dry buffalo chips lay thick on the ground here. Why was the fire so small? It could be that the leader of this revenge party was a foolish man. Or maybe," Kills Bear laughed again, "as Found Arrow suggested, one who liked traps."

Kit Fox held her breath with impatience. He must be getting near the interesting part, she thought.

"I crept nearer the fire, so near that grit from the cleared ground got under my leggings. A spark landed beside my head. Juniper wood. No sounds—the air was flat. Only the crackle of the fire broke the silence of the dark.

"I saw no sentries. I slipped around the fire. Circling further, I saw nothing. No enemy. Where was the revenge party?

"Behind me in the shadows a demon voice snickered."

The horse splashed sullenly through the water, and Kit Fox kicked at Found Arrow's ankle. Both of them recognized the demon creature of the war chief's story. Kills Bear with Knife continued. "Exactly at that moment the shape of a man started up from the ground in front of

48

me. My hand sought my knife. In one movement, as he rose to his feet, my blade pierced his breastbone. He was the only one, and when the dawn light came we understood it. From the pattern of his moccasins, and the bones shaping the lines of his face, we guessed him of the tribe of Snakes. I had not killed a Kootenai, but still, my knife had found an enemy.

"And his companion we captured—this one, this horse beside us." Kills Bear with Knife tugged on the lead.

The horse reared his head, golden against the shifting green-gray-brown scales of the river, and whinnied. He pranced his frustration. His hooves splashed lanceheads of the frigid river water. Kills Bear with Knife wound the lead around his wrist. They struggled with each other, the river water spraying around them. Water streamed over Kills Bear's face.

"I should have left him there!" yelled Kills Bear with Knife. "He will not obey me! He should have died with his master!"

Kit Fox said quickly, "You will ride him soon—"

"On the earth and the sky I promise you! He cannot be ridden."

"Except by his Snake master." Found Arrow's voice was strong and even.

The war chief's head swung away from them. Kit Fox guessed he would not admit there was anything the Snakes could do that the Bloods could not do. "Maybe the horse loved his Snake master," she suggested.

Kills Bear's lips pursed. His eyes punched holes in her. "Or maybe the horse feared him. Maybe the Snakes had tricks for taming horses that we have not found yet. But we will find them."

"This walking the horse in the water. This is a trick for taming him that you learned from some other tribe?" asked Found Arrow.

"From the Flathead tribe, that is so—from the Flathead warrior who came to trade nodules of obsidian. He also told me that the southern napikwan people sometimes starve their animals to make them trainable."

"Southern napikwan? Are those the white-faced men who wear the long black dresses?" asked Found Arrow.

"And talk about First Maker dying on a tree, and keep captive little yellow birds caged in their tipis, who sing when the napikwan order them. This Flathead trader traveled all the way south to them. I thought I would like to go and see that someday. They have many horses. They do not eat real meat, though. He said they only have meat from sweet-smelling, weak beasts that look like ghosts of buffalo." Kills Bear with Knife shook his head in disgust.

Found Arrow's eyes were wide with interest. He said, "Did the Flathead say it is true that some of them wear skins of iron?"

"And broil like meat on a spit, in the sun?" countered Kills Bear with Knife.

The men were absorbed in trading southern napikwan stories. Kit Fox listened with one ear. Her attention was on the horse who now trailed through the water behind them. If only Whiteweasel would interest himself in this animal! She longed for the wise advice that he, more than any other in their band, could give about animals.

50

But even her father did not care for the idea of the horse. The old ways were good. Why change them? And for guidance, his girls should go to their grandmother.

Old Holy Woman had advised Kit Fox not to trouble her father with her plans to ride the horse. But she was prepared to help Kit Fox's search for strength, in the way of their people. "Humble yourself," she told Kit Fox. "Ask holy assistance. Your vision was true. But though you must follow it, be open for new guidance as to where it will lead you. Only in this way can visions be used rightly for the people."

Old Holy Woman did not think they needed the horse. Their war chief, Kills Bear with Knife, did. As did Sun Smokes, and many of the other younger people. But even though the Blackfoot were among the most democratic of people, community opinion depended greatly upon the experience of the elders. How could the elders be expected to like something so new? Without the horse, what, in this world of new life, new weapons, new enemies, was to happen to her people?

A wet muzzle slid down her cheek, lipping her. She turned to look the horse in his huge brown eye. She thought, this creature seems able to see all of me with just one of his eyes.

Kills Bear with Knife apparently did not mind that the horse had come to nuzzle Kit Fox. His voice rose and fell on the riverbank; he seemed to be lecturing Found Arrow about the necessity of dealing with horses and about their stubbornness. They were even worse than dogs, he complained.

Kit Fox untangled a coil of her hair before any of it

could be destroyed by the yellow teeth, each longer than a joint of her finger. For the first time Eagle Flies Over Hills did not pull away from her. Were they to be friends? Tomorrow she wanted to ride him.

Found Arrow's hand on her shoulder interrupted them. "Do you remember this?" he asked, teasing, as he dangled some feathers in front of her.

It was the hair ornament, prairie chicken feathers flipping from a red and yellow quillworked band, that she had given him while they waited for Chief Kills Bear with Knife. She drew another from her pouch. This one had longer feathers attached to a plain buckskin band. Let Found Arrow dare tease her for her love of hunting! She would show them all she had both manly and womanly skills. "My mother says it is time for everyone to see my handiwork," she explained. She made the ornaments and gave them away. It was a way of showing the tribe her talent for handiwork.

Kills Bear with Knife hung the ornament solemnly from his hair. "I wondered why she wanted to walk with us by the river," he remarked to the younger man. "Not to hear an old man's stories! Her mother wants it known that Kit Fox is old enough to marry. To which of us do you think she will make the gift of moccasins?"

Kit Fox wished she could throw herself into the river and swim away from them. Why were men so unbearable sometimes? And why should she care? She did not like either of them! Her parents had never mentioned either as a husband for her. She did not want to marry anyone; leave that for Many Deer, who must worry about that kind of thing now she had passed her nineteenth

52

winter. Kit Fox could live carefree and happy in her parents' tipi, without any stupid husbands. She was only sixteen.

Found Arrow tittered. "From the expression on her face, I do not think she wants either of us! Mean-hearted woman!"

Kit Fox blushed, as Kills Bear with Knife leaned against Found Arrow and pulled their locks together to compare the two hair ornaments. Wheezing and cackling in the voice of an ancient, he pretended great distress. "Mine is longer—see, young man, even if she has worked yours in the holy craft, with such bright colors of porcupine quills. How much time did that take, child? My feathers are longer! How well done these are. She will be an excellent . . ." and he grinned wolfishly, "wife for someone. Did you say you had seen eighteen summers, Found Arrow? And no one yet to warm your tipi?"

Found Arrow waved his hand. "Kills Bear, there is nothing to blush for. Kit Fox is only a friend from my childhood, with an interest in horses and all other animals."

Kills Bear with Knife shot them each a warning glance. "And no interest in young men, eh, or in older ones. Well, then, I do not need to advise Old Holy Woman to hurry and see she is either chaperoned or married." Kit Fox knew the tradition to which he referred— once a girl became a woman, she would not be trusted alone except with brothers and those who might as well be brothers. She had not seen enough summers for that yet.

Shrill cries sounded from the camp path, and Kit Fox

turned to see where the noise came from. It was Cub, her next-to-youngest brother. The youngest still slept all day in Cub's old cradleboard. Usually Kit Fox was as glad to see him coming as she was to be leapt at by a flea, but at the moment his presence was acceptable. She fell to her knees and beckoned him and the little girl with him to pile on her for an exuberant hug. Soft bodies in her arms, she asked, "Why did you come? Did you want to tell me a secret?"

The little girl, Calf, lisped something around the finger in her mouth.

Kit Fox encouraged her. "Mother gave you some berry soup, yes. Can you take that finger out of your mouth and tell me what your secret is? Is that your secret?"

"Hi-yah, Chief Kills Bear with Knife!" burst out Cub. "We do not have any secret for this woman here," holding his plump and grubby hands together. "We have something special to tell everyone!"

The war chief's lips twitched. "We hear you. What is this great news you bear?"

Having won the attention of the great man, Cub was at first so overwhelmed he was unable to speak. "The buffalo have come," his voice whispered, awed at being the one to bring this message. "The owner of the beaver bundle has brought us the buffalo. A great herd of buffalo—hundreds, thousands, and Antelope Runner will lead them!"

They returned to a camp busy as a wild bees' nest in springtime. Men pulled cured wands of saskatoon wood one at a time through a bone straightener. The hunters would need quiverfuls of arrows.

Women assembled dog travois, dog harnesses, butchering tools, scrapers, buffalo paunches to line boiling pits, and the yapping scrawny yellow dogs and howling huge gray half-wolf dogs who must submit, in the end, to straps and leather webbings around their bellies. Children raced, playing tag between tipis, scattering dust. One toddler cried as he clung with pudgy arms to his mother's ankles. She glanced up at Kit Fox from the dog travois she was loading. Kit Fox knelt and untangled the baby and hugged him to silence.

Kit Fox found her bow and dragged it out by the flap of the tipi. If only she could reach the buffalo jump, her good-natured father probably would not bother to object.

"Daughter, what are you doing with a bow and quiver?"

That was her mother. Kit Fox was caught, half in and half out of the tipi. "I am only going up to the piskan. Like I did last time. These are my bow and quiver."

The old women and her mother and her sister knelt before the tipi fire. A delicate incense hung in the air. Already they had begun to burn the long coil of dried sweetgrass. They had begun their prayer vigil for the buffalo runner. They expected her to stay and join with the other grown women in prayer to First Maker. How could she not? They would think she did not care about Antelope Runner! But she had been so careful not to give him her promise.

Her mother's eyes gleamed, cold, shiny and black as obsidian.

Rarely had Kit Fox ever disagreed with her. But this time she felt she must. "I—will stay if you need me. But, you are all here already. Is the small power of my prayers

55

needed?" She begged. "Kills Bear with Knife worries there are not enough hunters at the corral who are fast with the bow. Bad Eyes told me."

Three Catcher sighed, her hand stroking nervously along the even stitches of her finely sewn shoulder cape. "Kit Fox, you are usually so wise for your age. Think of your duty, and do not whine like a baby."

Three Catcher was always bewildered and saddened by conflict, her daughter remembered.

"Mother, if you liked, I could take the skinning tools and a dog travois with me and leave them at the preparation field. When the messengers reached you from the jump to say the killing was over and it was time to start butchering, you would know there was one of us already working at the site." Kit Fox sighed at the thought of the blood, grease and gut-contents that would stain her hands and the front of her workdress. But it was necessary.

As her mother's eyes slid sideways as if to check Old Holy Woman's reaction, Cub spun through the tipi flap and into his mother's arms, his tears splattering onto his mother's buckskin skirts.

"Your foot is full of thorns!" his mother scolded. "What are they, cactus spines? You should not have been running barefoot."

Already Old Holy Woman was tossing bags of herbs out of their carrying-case, and Many Deer was heating water for a poultice. Cub's tears swelled to a downpour as his mother began pulling the spikes.

"Why were you not wearing your moccasins?" she demanded.

"It is indeed a good thing that you kept your leggings and your shirt on," Swift Hands Woman assured him, "or you would have cactus spines in so many more places."

The women chuckled. "Poor baby!" Kit Fox protested, as she slathered the ointment over the soles of Cub's feet. "Poor, pitiful one!" But Cub did not like the giggling of the women.

"Only the thought of how much worse you could have been hurt makes it funny," Many Deer explained as she stroked her brother's round forehead. He rolled his eyes at her. "We are so relieved. Do you feel well enough to think of other things now?" she continued. He stopped pouting.

"Father said I could bring his lance and the ax to the piskan." Cub sat up as he made the announcement. "He said I did not have to sit in the tipi and pray with a bunch of women."

"Cub! The huntmaster himself prays rather than joining in the hunt directly." Three Catcher frowned with her eyebrows, even though the rest of her still looked amused.

"Mother, Cub could never carry the lance and the ax all that way, and now his foot is sore. He should not be running on it. Can I go?" begged Kit Fox. She did not wait for discussion, but walked directly toward freedom.

"He said me, me!" were the last words she heard as she dashed out of earshot. "Not her—me!"

Kit Fox counted eighteen heads at the corral, all but herself and one other girl being older boys or menfolk. The fence had been rebuilt to a head taller than the tallest warrior, at the poundmaster's direction. So this fence loomed several heads higher than the pound corral where Kit Fox had shot while sitting on the edge, last autumn.

"Do not climb it," her father warned, pausing for a moment in his man talk. "Find a chink to send your arrows through."

Kit Fox sighed with relief. Whiteweasel had not questioned her being there; they needed all the help they could find. With Whiteweasel's acceptance, Kit Fox knew the other warriors would not question her either.

She squinted up at the cliff head, watching for the first sign of the buffalo. Bad Eyes and most of the women and smaller children were up there, hidden behind the drive lines to frighten the thundering buffalo, so they did not veer off before the jump. She prayed, May this herd not be lost. May no one be injured trying to turn them. May Antelope Runner be safe, and may he run well.

Already the rumble of a thousand hooves could be heard like a storm in the distance. The sound grew. Distant shrieks and war cries told the people at the corral that the herd had reached the narrowed drive lines, the last stage before the jump. The animals would be running shoulder against shoulder, driven and tormented by the screams of the people along the drive lines. Now Kit Fox thought she could hear the calves bawl, and their mothers answer. The earth, the air, the sky bellowed. She thought the bones of her head would cave under the sound.

The first cow spun from the drop. Hooves kicking at the sky, the massive stony weight of her skull hauled her

58

violently backward. At the last moment the hooves rolled for earth, but before the body could right itself it had smashed on the sharp-edged fallen rocks of the talus.

Another cow followed the lead buffalo. Immediately came more—cows, red-furred calves, a bull so large that the wall of the piskan shook at the moment of his landing. The buffalo were crashing around the lead cow's fractured corpse. It was, thought Kit Fox, as if they were the dark pieces of the sky itself, falling. None moved after they hit the ground. Silence held under the cliff, while overhead surged the shrieks of the terrified buffalo, pushed when they could see their doom by the force of hundreds of bodies behind them, thundering toward destruction. Kit Fox could only gape at the massive bodies tumbling above her. She knew in her gut that they were corpses already, even as they fought the uprushing ground in their frenzy.

Brown and tawny hulks hummocked the rock slope. Layers of buffalo. Kit Fox peered through her peephole in the piskan's woven branches at a new sight, a moving one, a snorting brown-black furry mask. Bloody red rimmed the buffalo's eyes: though not dead, she was wounded.

The fall must have damaged her hindquarters, maybe broken her back, or she would have been charging the piskan at three times her speed. Kit Fox could not pull her attention from the enormity of the furred forelegs, so powerful, dragging the smaller hindlegs behind them. The cloven hooves struck clots of yellow earth, laced with blood, hoof-holds driven into the floor of the piskan. For a moment Kit Fox stood frozen by pity. The girl started as someone jabbed an elbow into her ribs. She drew back her bowstring as calm as if she were in a vision, and let go her arrow, to free the beast from its terror.

"Good shot!" whooped Raven Tail Feathers, and she turned, as if awakening, to find him standing beside her. He added, "For a moment I thought you had not noticed the shooting had started."

He must have been the one who nudged me in the ribs so I would shoot the wounded buffalo, thought Kit Fox. Strange, why did he not take the shot himself? Raven smiled at her, as handsome as any man ever born, his throat's pulsebeat alive with excitement. Kit Fox was exhilarated by the danger.

The groans of several wounded buffalo echoed from the cliff wall, and she concentrated on the union between her mind and her arrows. In the background someone chanted a song of praise and gratitude to the chief of the buffalo. The people would honor the buffalo; the buffalo would forgive them; for the people needed the buffalo, even as the buffalo needed the grass of the prairie. The sacred powers had given so much food that even the people's old, their ill and their babies might survive the famines of winter. The people were thankful.

fur, as only a calf could have in autumn. As the shooter, his hide would come to her. A calf robe for Cub, her little brother, to wrap him and keep him warm through the frozen moons of winter: that had been her goal, and she had won it.

So had her people always lived, like eagle or wolf, in harmony with the universe. In her heart she gave thanks to the spirits of buffalo and deer, beaver and mink and marten. "So may my people live forever!"

If not for her people, the buffalo would shear the grass of the plains down to the roots—for no other creature hunted buffalo in any great number—and the dust would blow all over the world. Her grandmother said that. If not for the eagles, the ground squirrels and hares would nibble every green shoot, and there would be little food for the buffalo. Her grandmother said that. If not for the coyotes, the mice would consume all the seeds and nothing would grow on the plains in springtime. Her grandmother said that, too. All creatures had the places First Maker gave them, in the world's harmony.

The corral was silent now except for the moans of the remaining wounded. Kit Fox guessed these were the last of the herd; no more bodies fell to join their brothers. The band had enough. She hoped no people had been wounded. She took her last easy shots through the corral's opening. Then the young men climbed over with ax or lance or club in hand. Soon the huntmaster would come, to see that each hunter and each family had a fair share.

Raven Tail Feathers asked if she would like to use his bow while he ran down to the river for a drink. The southern osage wood inside the bow shone the color of sunlight just before sunset; the outer, sinewed side was backed with a rattlesnake skin. Like everything belonging to Raven, it was special.

He could not have offered Kit Fox anything to which she would have been more vulnerable. "The skin feels dry," she said as she took the bow in her hand.

"As my throat," he said and left.

She shook the bow to hear the sound of the five dangling rattlesnake rattles. Just then, war cries sounded again from overhead. Kit Fox located her father among the warriors sitting atop the corral to her right. He smiled at her, or at the bow she carried, but shrugged when she yelled her question, as if he could not hear over the noise. Her nearest neighbors were talking, a man and his woman. Kit Fox leaned across to the wife. Something caught her eye.

A body was falling from the top of the cliff.

A buffalo. A stray old bull that the people on the drive lines must have goaded. He fell feet forward, landing on bent knees on the stack of corpses, and then he was off. On all four unbroken feet, and running, he headed straight for Whiteweasel.

Whiteweasel raised his lance over his shoulder, balancing his left hand on the willow bark of the fence. A young warrior swung to cover him. The rest of the crowd held their breath. Two spearcasts away—now the lance thrust its power—and the snorting buffalo swerved for Kit Fox's hole in the fence.

The arrow, fitted to protect her father, left her bowstring by reflex. A boy screamed in the piskan as the bull crashed into the barrier. Splinters flew at Kit Fox's face as she dodged sideways.

But the barrier held. The warrior sitting beside Kit Fox yelled his war cry. She shuddered, recovering her breath for a moment, then joined the others climbing up on the barrier to see the end. The bull sank to his knees, blood bubbling from his nostrils, with a lance jutting from one eye socket. As soon as her knees stopped trembling she would congratulate the warrior who slew him. The red-banded arrow in the bull's neck was her shot. And the other arrow?

Its short shaft was circled by three yellow lines, and tufted with wild goose feathers trimmed close to cut like the wind. Antelope Runner's arrow.

So the buffalo runner had survived!

That night, orange-red firelight gleamed on the dancers' faces, revealing their exhilaration after the men's society ceremonies of the day. Kit Fox watched quietly, alone in the darkness of tipis ringing the dance area. She was not expecting anyone to search her out. Instead, she amused herself noticing how the firelight picked out a few features of each dancer. She recognized Antelope Runner by his hawk's beak of a nose. Found Arrow she spied easily. His height and slimness were matched by two other young dancers, but she knew him by the way he moved.

When the drums paused, she watched Raven Tail Feathers slip across the men's ring to talk with her sister. The lines of his body seemed to tighten even as his head bent toward her. For a moment their profiles caught the firelight. They look, she thought, like the hero man and hero woman of some ancient legend.

The drum began its beat again. Kit Fox stepped back into the shadows. She wanted to dance, but if she started dancing she would dance till gray dawn light. Even more than she wanted to dance she wanted to rise early and visit the horse. The horse was her greatest pleasure. Even greater than her sister or her friends.

As she stood in the cover of the tipis, she watched as one of the other warriors buffeted Found Arrow and laughed, punching at his shoulders. It was the warrior named Star; Kit Fox knew Found Arrow deserved it. The story was that Found Arrow had handed Star prairie crocuses to wipe himself with when they were hunting on the prairie last spring. Star trusted his friend and used them. When his skin started to peel in awkward places, he laughed along with everybody else. But now Found Arrow had to accept, with equal good humor, the revenge for his practical joke.

A hand patted Kit Fox's arm. It was Song Sparrow, Many Deer's closest friend, who lived in the tipi in front of which Kit Fox stood. "Kit Fox? Are you enjoying the dance?" she asked. "I am not used to seeing you standing by yourself."

Kit Fox said, "I was watching the dancers." The next dance would be women in one ring and men in the other. Somewhere in the darkness a woman's voice lifted in heart-stirring song.

Song Sparrow stomped her feet in the movement of the dance. "I want to join this one. But my baby is alone in the tipi. It would not be good to leave him there.

What would you do, Kit Fox? I suppose I should stay. I really cannot leave him by himself." She swayed in time to the music.

Kit Fox shivered. Found Arrow looked in her direction; she wondered if he saw her. Perhaps she should walk over and greet him. Probably, she thought, he saw her and did not want to be with her. Just like her father, always busy with his friends.

"I will look after your baby, Song Sparrow," she said.

"For two dances?"

Found Arrow was looking her way again. But he did not move. Was he really her friend? She told Song Sparrow, "Yes."

She ducked quickly into the tipi. But she thought that out of the corner of her eye she had seen him walking toward her.

When she had checked the baby, she peeked out through the tipi flap. No Found Arrow in sight. Now she would never know whether he would have talked to her. She wished she could call the chance back. If he came near again then she might step out for a moment, ask him if he was enjoying the dance. Song Sparrow's baby hung asleep in his cradleboard. Kit Fox decided to sit by the tipi flap and watch, and then when Found Arrow came she would swing outside, confident and casual as if she were Many Deer. Kit Fox looked carefully at everybody dancing on her side of the fire to make out the features of each as they moved into the glare from the charcoal-colored night.

Two silhouettes of women drifted to stand in the dark by the door. When they began to gossip about ceremonial clothes and the elks' teeth decorations, Kit Fox's skin twitched with irritation. After a time she recognized the low laughter of the war chief's oldest daughter. The other, the sharp little whisper, was a voice she could not identify, though something about it was familiar.

The sharp little whisper said, "Yours will be a fine dress, people should notice it, but maybe they will only be thinking about Many Deer's dress."

No, thought Kit Fox. Many Deer has made an enemy. More than one woman was jealous of her sister's beauty and cleverness. Sometimes Kit Fox was jealous herself. But this woman sounded as if she would let jealousy drive her to mean revenge. Kit Fox watched the chief's daughter with concern. "What do you mean?" the chief's daughter asked. "Many Deer does not own a ceremonial dress."

"She will have a new dress for when she goes to her husband."

"Certainly. That is a proper time for a Blood woman to have a new dress."

"You would never begrudge her—we know that, you are generous," continued the hiss.

"I hear what you say."

More and more words poured out. "You are so generous with the pretty Many Deer. You said nothing yesterday, when she won too often for her team, playing the hand game. Winning and winning. No one ever won that much before."

"Aiii. It is true. I lost a roseberry necklace in the gambling, myself."

"But did she say, 'It is just luck from that dream I

67

dreamed last night?' Did she take care to lose at the end?"

Again the shadow on the left nodded. "I hear this also, that you say."

"You hear me because you are so generous. But even of generosity there can be enough, too much. You are generous, you will be generous, no matter how often Many Deer's father speaks in council, even though the beaver bundle he owned has been sold to your father. No matter if Antelope Runner is chosen to lead the buffalo—you applaud him, you are generous. When they say how handsome he is, you are kind. But generous as you are, can you admit that you owe none of them any kindnesses? And as for Kit Fox—"

"I had not thought of this. No. Except—the scraping knife Many Deer lent me this spring. And the time Old Holy Woman made the right medicine to cure my cough. Then Antelope—"

"Only you are so generous you would remember such tiny things! I ask," and the one with the sharp voice leaned close, her hand touching her friend's back, "do you not think they would have done the same for anyone?"

Kit Fox wanted to interrupt them, say something to defend her family. She felt ill with dislike. Suddenly she guessed who the person with the snaky voice was as it continued, "Do you know who Many Deer sews a pair of moccasins for? Raven Tail Feathers!"

"Do you not think him good enough for her?"

"Him for her?! Her for him!"

The chief's daughter laughed again, as she had at the

beginning of the conversation. "You wanted to marry Raven yourself, Took Two Lance, did you not? It is no shame to admit it."

She put her arm around Took Two Lance and they walked back to the dance. I will tell Many Deer about her enemy tomorrow, Kit Fox thought. Tomorrow is soon enough—and we will think about what to do, and then I am sure we will laugh.

CHAPTER SIX

Early morning sun lit the meadow. The sky shone pale blue, dotted with rabbit's tail clouds. Never in her life had Kit Fox been more happy. Her arms circled the horse's chest like a necklace. Eagle Flies Over Hills rocked beneath her, his dusty, short sleek fur so warm against her legs.

She caressed the ponokamita's nose. She stroked two fingers in a stripe between his eyes down to his great round nostrils. He wriggled them out of shape.

"Found Arrow, watch. He makes strange shapes with his nostrils whenever the end of my sleeve comes near them."

"Maybe he does not like the way you smell."

"He did not at all mind the old dress I wore yesterday."

The strong smoke smell of her new dress did repel mosquitoes. She rubbed it across the shoulders of Eagle Flies Over Hills.

"Do you not think you have been here long enough for today?" Found Arrow asked.

"Are you afraid someone will see me? You will tell them it was not me they saw, it was the shadow of that thundercloud overhead." Kit Fox could not bear to leave. Now that she had learned the beast's ways he seemed pleased to have her ride him.

"You did not talk to me last night at the dance, Kit Fox, but here you are this morning, now that I am guarding the horse again."

Ah, Kit Fox thought, he expected me to find him. But she did not want to offend him. "Found Arrow?" Kit Fox tilted her head so her hair slid down the neck of the horse. It was embarrassing to say the words. "I did want to talk to you, but I was watching Song Sparrow's baby. I really am grateful to you."

Found Arrow stopped suddenly, so suddenly that the horse bumped against his back. Eagle Flies Over Hill swung his head; his eye rolled back to question Kit Fox.

Whatever she expected Found Arrow to say, she did not predict his announcement. "That hill is it!" They had walked downstream, east from the horse meadow to where the riverbanks hardly crested at all. Now Found Arrow nodded at a mound several arrow flights beyond the bank, on the prairie itself. A rock outcrop broke from its side, and tufts of low-growing juniper stuck out like an old man's uncombed hair.

Kit Fox queried, "That hill is what?"

"That hill is my eagle pit. For catching the eagle with my hands, so I can make my war shield."

She could see nothing special, though she scanned the

hill carefully. She shivered; the puffs of clouds blowing over the hill had turned gray. Found Arrow might be seeing something outside her range of sight. But he did not say what.

A brown bird perched on a poplar branch to their right cocked its head in a fast trill, then back again. He sang, "fee-bee, fee-bee, fee-bee." But Found Arrow did not even seem to hear the bird. He continued, "This pit took me three mornings to dig. First with pointed sticks to break up the earth, and then with a buffalo's shoulder blade, shoveling it. By the time I finished I was tired enough to fall into it!"

They tied up the horse and climbed to the eagle pit. The juniper branches bent slippery under their weight as they climbed.

Found Arrow knelt to brush the dull green plumes that spilled over the edge of the pit. "Next I will weave a webbing of willow branches as we did for the corral. Then I will lace the juniper through the holes, so the evergreen branches are fixed solidly, and so every branch slants away from the center at an angle—see? Like the tail on a ruffled grouse when he spreads it for courtship. That is the way the juniper grows. To the eye of the eagle overhead, it will seem to grow naturally."

"If I were an eagle, I would think it natural. I could not see it at all until you showed me," Kit Fox told him. She thought she saw Found Arrow flush under his skin then, or was it only that they had been climbing in the heat of the sun? He did seem embarrassed; all modesty appeared to have left him when he showed her his work.

"How much weight can such a cover take on top of

it?" she continued. "If I were an eagle, what would happen when I jumped on it?"

She flapped her arms and screeched, "Hi-yah! I am a giant, mean old mother eagle. And you are glad I am a mother eagle because a mother is bigger than a father eagle and you want the longest feathers you can catch—"

Found Arrow's face became serious. "When the spirits have answered my prayers, when in some form First Maker is shown me in vision—then I shall fasten the eagle feathers onto my war shield." He flung his arms open to the winds of his dreams. "Feathers for my shield!"

"And also—"

"Legbones to make flutes so I may play for First Maker many tunes."

"And also—"

"Feathers for ornaments to tie to my hair and my lance."

"And?"

"Feathers to tie to my friends' hair?"

"And feathers for fletching your good friends' arrows!"

"Whose arrows?" His voice squeaked with astonishment.

"My arrows, too. Am I not one of your good friends?"

"Yes, Kit Fox. But you are a woman."

"Do you mean I cannot be your friend or that I should not fletch arrows?" she asked.

"A Blood warrior does not have women for friends. He has his warrior friends. At home he has women who are relatives, and he has his wife. Only an old man might have an old woman for a close friend . . ." Found Arrow

73

shook his head in confusion. "Otherwise people will think she is something else."

"Is that why you did not want me to visit the horse?" Kit Fox asked. She almost yelled at him. "You are afraid they will think *that* of us?"

He did not answer.

"I am only sixteen," she continued to protest. "My older sister is nineteen, and she is not married yet. I am not yet fully a woman. You are not married, and you are eighteen."

"We are young. But if they see us together often, they will tell tales." Found Arrow paused, and added, "Your sister is marrying, is she not?"

Kit Fox swung a loose willow branch at a bald patch on the ground. Furry creatures ran, their passages tiny rivulets in the grass. Kit Fox thought, so Found Arrow does not want to be my friend because his brother Raven might be marrying Many Deer. Probably he expects me to be a co-wife to Raven Tail Feathers. Everyone else seems to.

"I do not have to marry him!" she cried. "I have a right to say no."

"Sorry," Found Arrow said.

The wind battered the junipers on the hill. She cleared her throat. "I am still too young," she offered. "Not much too young, just enough too young. I do not want to bear children yet and toil all day as a wife must. That is difficult work. When I am old enough to be married I will want to work hard and well."

"Courage, long-suffering, skill, strength, endurance—"

"I pray to have all of those," said Kit Fox.

74

Found Arrow pursed his lips for a moment, then moved jerkily back to pry off the top of his eagle trap. He jumped down so he was crouched in the pit. Catching the change of mood, Kit Fox was quick to slide the willow web and juniper boughs over his head. As she lay down on her belly, the better to peer through the mesh at him, she said, "Now will you agree to give me the littlest feathers for my arrows?"

Their giggles released the tension at the top of Kit Fox's stomach. Found Arrow's answer was, "Of course. Though you have never explained to me why you want to tip your arrows with golden eagle feathers."

She smiled to herself. "I want them because they are the best. Do you not know how good a shot I am? Raven Tail Feathers himself loaned me his snakeskin bow at the buffalo jump."

Her companion's voice sounded flat and weary. "Yes, Raven Tail Feathers. At least when he marries your sister, you and I may still talk as friends."

"I hope we can be friends always." A stone sat in her stomach; it was the first time she had admitted that to herself and to Found Arrow.

"Let me up." Found Arrow clambered out of the trap and walked around its edge, avoiding Kit Fox's body as if she were an obstacle like one of the rocks. He shook each leg in turn, perhaps checking to be certain that once the cramps were gone, they would still work.

He had seemed not to hear her. Kit Fox drew a deep breath and continued, "But I am not sure you wish to be the friend of anyone in my family. Someone has been telling mean stories about Many Deer."

75

"Someone is telling tales about Many Deer? From jealousy? Or has she offended them?"

"Both, I guess," admitted Kit Fox.

"Jealousy, I would expect. But you must understand with how much cause they are jealous of her. If you were as widely known and as pretty as she is and did the things you do, some people would be jealous."

Kit Fox flinched from his words. It was all so unfair and so troubling. Why did everybody always have to remind her of how pretty her older sister was?

"Have I ever compared you to Raven Tail Feathers?" Kit Fox protested. "My friends know I am a healer—I understand the ways of plants and animals. I design beautiful patterns. My friends like me for that. And because I help them call live eagles to their hands." Now she felt better.

She thought she saw a little hurt on his face, so after a moment's silence, she went on, "For the eagle trap, we need a wolfskin, an awl, and some sinew for sewing." Found Arrow scuttled down the hill without saying another word. Kit Fox was relieved that he did not answer. She watched him until he was out of sight. Overhead, a storm was building.

She checked her snares downstream, past where they had tied the horse. By nose alone she knew one deadfall triggered by a skunk. The next deadfall upwind had crushed the skull of a porcupine. She gutted and cleaned it, neat and quick with her knife. She wrapped the porcupine liver in leaves and tucked it into her pouch. She could safely leave the carcass to hang from a branch above grizzly bear reach. The remaining innards were buried under a hand's-breadth of rotting leaves.

If only she could have brought them back for the dogs to devour. Poorer cousins of the wolves, the camp dogs had surrendered independence in favor of reliance on what humans chose to give them—sometimes much, and sometimes little. Kit Fox's own favorite, a yellow mutt with a black-tipped tail, loved long runs with her over the prairie. She admitted her mother's complaint that he did not run nearly as well once harnessed to a travois. Pot-scrapings, intestines and bones were feasts to him. Why waste on dogs food that might be needed later by children? Life was hard enough on the prairie.

When Kit Fox came back for the porcupine, some of it would be for her small furry one. Summer was no famine time; better to fatten her dog now so he might stay healthy through the moons of cruel biting snow that would ice his paws in winter.

When Found Arrow returned, Kit Fox was lying on the grass by the eagle trap, arms curled against the wind. Together they pulled dried stems, brush and twigs for stuffing the wolfskin. Kit Fox punched holes around the edge with the awl. Then they plumped out the belly with vegetation; she sewed it shut, using the sinew.

She apologized. "I am afraid the legs and tail have to dangle."

"The eagle will see him as a long-dead wolf, belly bloated, legs rotten. Good bait. Do not worry. Is this not the way your father said it was done?" Found Arrow reassured her.

"At least it does not smell that bad. Father said it was one of the ways. You now know many different ways to trap the eagle. But this is the surest one."

"Well, this wolf looks quite dead, all right. Can we get the horse and head back to camp now?"

"Not yet. What do you think is an eagle's favorite food?"

Found Arrow snorted. "Mice? Hares? Babies? Dead wolves?"

"No, no, no and no."

"Tell me. We have been out here too long. I want to get back to the tipis. Your mother will be watching for you."

"Do you not want to guess what I have in my pouch here, just because I am a good friend and I want to help you?" Kit Fox did not care if she did not go back to the camp soon. "Watch carefully," she teased, "and I will show you what an eagle desires—"

Her friend leaned forward, and she spoke in his ear, "Stinky porcupine liver!"

"That is what an eagle desires?" squawked Found Arrow.

"Certainly. Except he will think it is wolf liver. If you wait a moment, I can sew it to the wolfskin, so the eagle will think it is hanging out." Her hands moved squeamishly on the messy job. "There. He will see it and— whoosh! down, before another eagle can grab his tidbit. He will fly into your hands, for certain."

"Soon," said Found Arrow. "You will have to come and watch what I do then."

"Tell me the day."

They both laughed.

"Kit Fox? Where were you? Midmorning, and you have not filled the water bags," scolded Swift Hands Woman from the back of the tipi. Kit Fox saw with concern that the old lady still lay on her sleeping couch.

"I was with the horse."

"With who?"

"With some friends," the girl said quickly.

"Doing what? Why can you youngsters not leave that beast to Chief Kills Bear with Knife? He is dangerous. Night after night I dream of napikwan, of thunder and lightning over a battlefield, of young men dying," the old woman told her. The slits of her eyes blinked as she peered at Kit Fox. She lifted herself on one stringy arm. "The ponokamita brings great trouble for our people."

"The ponokamita brings great joy for our people," Kit Fox maintained, but with eyes downcast.

"Or maybe both." Old Holy Woman stood just inside the tipi, her hand wrapped around a stone knife. Her smile stretched across her face and shone in her eyes.

CHAPTER SEVEN

The next morning, as the wind-streaked dawn clouds reddened to rose, Found Arrow, Kit Fox, and some helpers finished his trap. The site he had chosen was near enough to the shaggy eagle's nest on a river bluff ledge so that one or both of the eagles flew over it most days. It was far enough from the nest so that preparation of the trap might go unnoticed. Now the time came for Found Arrow to bet the strength of his hands against the eagle's claws.

His mother and sisters promised to pray as they worked, for as many days as he risked his life. Hoping to keep him safe from talons and slashing beak, they would not touch knife or arrow, lance or awl till he returned safely. The thought of their love shielded his heart as he climbed the hill.

The first eagle came in midmorning. He saw the carcass, and spiraled down to see better, riding the breeze, his wingtips spread like fingers to catch the sky. Kit Fox bit her lip at the sight of him. She was glad she had not cried out—she did not want to startle the children who watched with her from the clump of aspen trees at the base of the hill. She imagined Found Arrow waiting in the trap, where she had left him earlier.

As soon as she saw the eagle, she knew he was a male. She knew because he was so small for his breed. As he dived, his shape could be fixed against the tops of the trees. He was about four hands long, his wingspread the length of a tall man from head to foot. His neck feathers and leg feathers shone golden brown next to the dull brown of head and body.

When his shadow covered her, she flinched in sudden fear.

Even after the sunshine folded warm again around her, she shivered, her heart pounding at the omen of death, of the eagle's death. Found Arrow she knew to be strong and brave—no eagle's beak would rend his eyes, no claws gouge life out of him. There was no reason for her to be afraid.

The children giggled beside her. Calf forgot all caution and whooped with joy as the eagle's claws sank into the bait carcass. Kit Fox hushed her with the palm of her hand, her vision fixed on Found Arrow's trap. "If you will not stay still and be quiet, I will have to take you back to camp. Remember, you promised your mother you would be quiet."

Now, Found Arrow had the bird by the feet. Its great wings flapped—a hooked bill tore the sky in anguish. As the wind rattled the leaves at the top of the grove, Kit Fox hugged Calf's body to her chest, stilling her. Would Found Arrow keep his grip?

The bird's beak cut into Found Arrow's arm, still holding him. Found Arrow jerked him down. Now the eagle struggled to keep his breast from tearing on the edges of the trap, and his wings wrenched upward. Another tug. Kit Fox watched the bird's neck stretch in a desperate cry. Then he vanished from her sight.

She held her breath for a moment, then ran up the slope toward Found Arrow. As she reached the top of the hill, a cloud covered the sun and she was slapped by a blast of wind. Not a sound came from the pit.

The children had followed her. "Stay back," she yelled at them. They crouched in the juniper.

Found Arrow was an ugly sight as he rose from the eagle pit. A talon had traced a line in blood from his mouth to his jawbone, a moon-shaped blood talisman. Blood ran from his fingers and from jagged gouges in his knees. But he had lost no strength with the blood.

"I am stronger than the eagle!" Found Arrow cried. He pulled a ragged lump of feathers up from the hole. "I pressed him under my knees, crushed the back of his skull beneath my fist."

Cub came close and touched the carcass with one finger, his other hand in his mouth, his eyes dark round bowls filled with delight. Calf crept nearer with her arm drawn back and one hand wrapped around a rock.

"No, Calf," Found Arrow begged. "Do not throw it. He is dead, and I want the feathers whole. If there are enough feathers." He laughed into Kit Fox's eyes.

"One will not be enough. I need more," he told her. "At least, his mate. She should fly over soon, looking for the eagle I have taken. Kit Fox, you and the children should take cover."

For the remainder of the morning the children patiently drowsed as they had been trained to do when stalking animals. At midday, Kit Fox looked up to see the outline of the eagle's mate, black against the thundercloud.

Twice the she eagle rode down the gusts for a closer view of the decoy wolf. She must have been on her route home; her claws grasped prey for feeding her eaglets.

"Big," said Calf. Kit Fox nodded agreement. The body of this one stretched maybe as long as a warrior's lance. The span of her wings was greater than the height of the tallest warrior.

Calf cried when Kit Fox insisted she stay in their blind at the base of the hill. Her whole hope was to see Found Arrow capture the eagle. "Last time we were so far away it was all fuzzy. And then we had to run and run and when we got there—"

"Found Arrow had already killed him. Without us!" Cub completed her sentence. His cheeks flushed with indignation. "If we had been there, we could have helped him."

Patiently his sister reminded them, "We dare go closer, but not so close that our smell will come to the eagle. We did not clean our bodies with the sweetgrass smoke. The proper ceremonies were not held for us. We are not ready." She did not remind them of the danger. Danger would just be more temptation.

Cub stared at the hilltop, his lower lip rigid. His sister guessed he was imagining himself in Found Arrow's position.

Calf still protested. She banged the stone in her hand

against a soft yellow sandstone set in the ground. "We all washed in the river this morning! You were there. I rubbed mud on your back. Remember?"

"You did, you brown weasel. And I splashed you!" Kit Fox loved her brother's playmate. She saw in her the younger sister she might have had; but none had been born into her tipi and lived. She sighed. "To please you then, we will dare just a little more danger."

Cub cried, "We can hide in those bushes!"

At Kit Fox's reluctant agreement, he set off toward the clump of buckbrush at the foot of the hill, wriggling through the wind-blown dry grasses, all tangled with the year's new growth. Kit Fox was pleased to see him creep as close to the ground and silent as a sparrow. The grass-color of his buckskin clothing hid him from the view of any cruel eyes. Calf had not learned her friend's camouflage skills, but ran with flailing arms and feet, awkward and easily seen.

"Belly down, head down," hissed Kit Fox. "What if a Snake warrior watched you? What if the eagle saw?"

In the shade of the buckbrush they set their eagle watch. Sometimes the sun escaped the clouds; between blasts of wind they sheltered in its warmth. At those times Kit Fox almost slept. Why should the eagle alight for a dead, mangy wolf? Ground squirrels and rabbits littered the long grass, juicy and easily caught. Why should Found Arrow insist on a second eagle? Kit Fox wished her friend to go home, while he still had both his eyes. One battle scar was enough.

Always she watched the sky. Which would arrive first, the storm or the eagle's mate?

Now the air slapped moist against her face, charged

with the coming storm's excitement. Kit Fox shook her head as the eagle dropped through buffeting wind currents. Broad wings spread against the sky; a female.

Cub and Calf squeaked and nudged each other in excitement as the eagle spiraled down. Claws spread to slice the air. How terrifying she looked, legs stretched wide in unchallenged power.

She struck. At the moment of collision, her beak seized the liver. Then she thrust upward for freedom.

But the liver was sewn down. The eagle's wings bobbed in an uneven half beat, uncertain. A hand shot out from under her, stretched to wrap itself around the mighty legs. She squawked in sudden alarm. The liver slipped from her mouth.

Her wings fought to free her. For a few flaps she hung suspended; she threw her head back and screeched her defiance. Even as she shrilled her cry, Found Arrow grabbed her other leg. The eagle had lost her main chance for freedom.

Kit Fox clenched her hands so hard that her fingernails gashed her skin. She heard Found Arrow cry out. She pressed her eyes shut, and with all her strength she prayed for her friend's victory. "Give him endurance. Do not let the eagle devour him. Give him strength to make this offering, First Maker."

Calf's shrill scream tore her eyelids open.

Kit Fox jumped to her feet. The children were scattering up the slope before her and without thinking, Kit Fox ran after.

"Found Arrow! Arrow!" Cub sobbed, as he raced to try and help his friend.

"Stop, Cub! Calf! Stop!" cried Kit Fox.

Calf ran silently ahead of them, toward Found Arrow, her path as straight as if she had been shot from a bow. Kit Fox reached for Cub. He was so near! As she felt his shoulder under her hand she forced herself past him, pushing him so he sprawled to the ground. Now here was Calf. Kit Fox caught the rawhide fringe across the girl's back. From the peak of the hill the eagle spoke.

The wind wailed with her. Now at last, the sky opened and sleet slashed down. Kit Fox realized she could not hold her grip with the wind pulling at her. With the next gust of wind, Calf tore away.

Kit Fox staggered and fell on one knee, her hands striking the ground. One hand clawed up a large rock. With her other hand she shielded her eyes to peer into the storm. She was the length of a lance throw from the hill's height, almost to level ground. She saw Calf throw herself upon the giant bird straining against the pit cover and the man below.

As Calf attacked the eagle, Found Arrow lost his hold and the eagle turned on Calf. For a moment Kit Fox hoped Found Arrow would now be able to escape the pit. But no—two bodies, eagle's and child's, now weighted the pit cover down.

The great wings surged above Calf. The eagle's claws were hooked in the belly of Calf's rawhide dress. And Calf fought. As Kit Fox watched, Calf punched and kicked at the eagle's underside. Suddenly Cub appeared and dragged at the back of Calf's dress, trying to pull her free.

Kit Fox weighed the stone in her hands as she raised herself against the storm's force. How could she throw without hitting the children? Yet there was no other choice.

The cover of the pit shook as Found Arrow again thrust upward. It was held down by children, eagle, and decoy, but still it jerked and slid. The sleet ended; light dropped like a net. When the eagle raised her head to scream, Kit Fox threw the stone. It hit.

At that moment Found Arrow thrust aside the trap cover. Cover, eagle and children tumbled over to rest precariously on the low juniper branches edging the pit. Hoisting himself up, Found Arrow set one foot on the eagle's head and the other upon her wing.

Again Cub tried to pull Calf to safety. Talons raked Calf, and she screamed. Kit Fox leapt to jab her foot into the eagle's feathered gut. The children rolled away. Then Kit Fox felt Found Arrow's arm slide around her waist, and lift her away from the eagle.

She shut her eyes in relief. Then she watched as Found Arrow gripped the eagle's feet, and whirled her overhead. As he shrilled his battle cry, he dashed the bird's head against a rock and crushed her braincase.

It was over. There were no sounds except the wind flattening the grass, and a small child's wailing. Kit Fox lifted Calf's head onto her lap.

"Is Calf—" her younger brother blurted, "is she—"

"Hush. Hush." She pressed her hands against Calf's stomach. "Could you hold Cub, Found Arrow?" Kit Fox maintained a steady pressure, but still the blood trickled out under her wrists. Rivulets ran down the hill to soak into the grass roots.

Found Arrow demanded, "Press harder!"

She bit her lip. "Get me your robe. Get your robe! I need something to bind that wound or the life will bleed out from her."

Found Arrow's eyes tracked wildly across the landscape. "By a rosebush. I dropped it somewhere between a big rock and a rosebush."

"I will find it," offered Cub. He dashed away.

Kit Fox stroked Calf's small, square forehead; the perspiration that dewed the gray-brown skin was cool to her touch. The child's eyelids flickered. Even that return of consciousness was enough return of pain to make her moan.

"Ah," breathed Found Arrow. "She is still alive."

At camp, Found Arrow carried Calf to her parents' tipi while Kit Fox found Old Holy Woman. Kit Fox rattled out the story to her grandmother's ears and they hunted through the medicine bags. "Calf spilled a bowlful of blood on the earth, but life is still beating strong in her," she concluded.

Old Holy Woman asked, "The eagle did not tear her face? Or into her chest? Or her belly?"

"Nothing—I saw no wounds on her face. Her belly is torn but not opened. She breathed no blood from her mouth or nose."

"We can ease her pain and help her heal."

Calf's father stood by their tipi door, his face made even more handsome and dignified by grief. "I am sorry," said Kit Fox. "The children ran from me when the eagle landed. Calf attacked it. There was little I could do."

"Calf will heal. But why were the children there? Were they trying to rescue Found Arrow?"

"Yes." The sight of his pain seared Kit Fox.

True to the Blackfoot understanding of fate, Calf's father did not waste time blaming, accusing, or demanding more details. "I will fetch a mighty spirit healer," he told them.

Old Holy Woman's feet were already directed toward the tipi flap. She paused only to reassure. "We will do whatever can be done to stop the blood flow with herbs, then welcome the spirit healer when he or she comes. Move quickly, Kit Fox."

Calf's mother looked up over Calf's body as they entered. She is very young, thought Kit Fox, and admired how she kept her presence of mind despite the tears welling in her eyes. Old Holy Woman handed her granddaughter some leaves of the gopher's ears plant. "Chew them," she commanded.

The old lady smiled at Kit Fox's willing obedience. Old Holy Woman pushed her gray hair from her face, then bent over her patient. A cloud grew in the back of the aged eyes as she scanned the child's injuries. Raising her hands over Calf's belly, she began her chant.

Calf jerked at the touch of the poultice. "It burns me!"

Her mother laughed and stroked her cheek. "Ah, you are going to heal! The medicine's sting has wakened you and brought you back to us. You need the leaf poultice to stop the flow of blood. I will hold your hand so you will not mind the hurt so much." Kit Fox shifted herself to make a better place for Calf's mother.

Even in the tipi's dim light, the girl could see how red still seeped through the crushed green of the leaves. Old Holy Woman reassured the others by the calmness of her removal of the poultice and her examination of the claw marks. She wrapped another strip of buckskin into a bandage; soon the bleeding stopped entirely.

"Stay with Calf," she ordered her granddaughter. "Swift Hands Woman is in the doorway. I must speak with her."

The other old lady tipped her head shyly as she joined them. She apologized, "A sad day, this one. Found Arrow and I have come to sit with the child until the spirit healer arrives. Found Arrow?"

Kit Fox noticed he left the tipi flap swinging loose behind him as he entered. His face seemed set, grim. He spared one glance for the child limp on the sleeping couch.

"Old Holy Woman," he stated respectfully, "we have come to fetch you where the need for you is even greater than the need here."

"I hear you, Found Arrow. Tell me your news; is someone in my family hurt?"

"Your family are well. No, you are called to tend the warriors Cuts Buffalo and Many Hill Walker. A Snake war party caught them as they rode back from their trip to the Peigans."

"They are badly hurt?" Old Holy Woman asked, her hands drawing shut the thong that closed her medicine pouch.

Found Arrow admitted, "Even if you come now, it may be that neither of them will live. The Snakes chased them. Three Bloods, running on foot, against six men on horseback—what chance did they have?" He ground his teeth in frustration. "The Snakes killed Star Child."

"We must be glad that two returned to our camp," Swift Hands Woman insisted, her voice resolute.

"Yes. If they live," said Found Arrow.

"Help me haul my aged bones to these warriors," Old Holy Woman demanded. Kit Fox offered her hands to raise her. The girl managed an inward smile at her grandmother's spirit, cantankerous and commanding even in bad times.

Swift Hands Woman sighed. "Aiii, my sister!" Old Holy Woman offered her arm to her co-wife. As Found Arrow took Swift Hands Woman's other arm, the old lady looked back at Kit Fox. "You will tend the child?"

"Of course she will," grunted Old Holy Woman.

"I meant, through any move we must make because of the Snake people. A hard, hard trail for a sick child— and for some of us old ones. But Kit Fox will help. She is growing into a strong-hearted young woman." Swift Hands Woman smiled at Kit Fox with the radiant grace of her inner confidence, and in the warmth of that smile Kit Fox felt herself grow toward her own strength.

CHAPTER EIGHT

F ound Arrow! See me fly like a hawk!" Kit Fox urged the horse to a gallop.

They picked up speed past where Found Arrow stood with his hands on his hips, and drove down the trail to the far end of the meadow. Kit Fox clung to the horse's neck with both her hands. She yipped her exhilaration.

As they neared the further trees she sighed, straightened a little to slow Eagle Flies Over Hills and turned him from the trail. The horse picked his way back through the tangled vetch and shoulder-high grasses to the meadow center and the man who waited.

Kit Fox slid down to join him. "I felt like a spirit of the wind, Found Arrow. I want you to know how that feels."

"It is time for the horse to obey me, too," agreed Found Arrow. But he was grinning.

Kit Fox smiled back, aware of her flushed face and the fast, ragged sound of her breathing. She handed over the horse's lead. "Your turn to ride," she said. "Or to be thrown—do you remember my first try?"

"I will not be thrown."

He probably will not be thrown, Kit Fox thought, as she reached past him to stroke Eagle Flies Over Hills. Or if he is, he will just get back on his feet and try again. She had come to have a great respect for Found Arrow. "I want to gallop the horse again tomorrow morning," she bargained.

And Found Arrow laughed.

On the center of the horse's nose grew a whirl of fur. It was like a wild sunflower, shining golden in the next day's early morning sunlight. If Kit Fox rubbed him there he would blow air at the side of her face and reach to nibble at her hair.

Found Arrow laughed when she shied away. "Do you not like his response?" he teased.

He wore her small gift of friendship, the hair ornament, she noticed. The eagle feathers cascaded down the edge of his cheek and his throat. They looked startling against the blue-black of his hair.

"I want the horse to stand very calmly," she said. "Just stand here in his meadow. Then he will not buck when you mount him." She stroked along the length of the horse's jawline. "I would like my eyelashes to be curly like the horse's."

"But then you would have those whiskers he has sticking out from his cheekbones," said Found Arrow.

"Whiskers!" she giggled.

"And that chin!" Found Arrow exclaimed.

"Be more serious."

"If you like." He warned, "Hold the horse still."

Found Arrow leaned his full weight on Eagle Flies Over Hills. It looked to Kit Fox as if he was concentrating. She watched shadows of the nearby trees play on his face. Finally he swung himself up onto the horse's back.

Kit Fox let her breath out slowly, so she would not disturb the horse. But Eagle Flies Over Hills only shivered once under his new burden. He chomped his giant yellow teeth at her. She let enough slack into the reins that he could bend and crop the grass.

"I want to try leading the horse forward," she said after a moment. They paced slowly toward the center of the meadow. "You ride more easily than I did, my first time."

Found Arrow laughed. "I was able to watch you. You did it without anyone to show you how."

They stopped by the wild rosebushes, with their new buds. Summer was coming, as certain as roses.

Kit Fox said, "It is not so difficult."

"What?"

"Riding. Is it?"

"You just have to take the risk and do it."

Kit Fox could tell how pleased Found Arrow was by his success. She thought how he would soon go alone into the wilderness to seek his spiritual helper, as the young men did, and dared to ask, "Is it the same way with the vision quest?"

"Yes."

"You are going soon?"

"As soon as the band reaches the summer camp in the Eagle Hills. And we begin the march to the camp tomorrow. So—"

A voice bellowed, "Kit Fox! What are you doing here without a chaperone?"

It was Kills Bear with Knife, the war chief. And Antelope Runner, and Raven Tail Feathers, striding in single line into the clearing from the westward path. Kit Fox realized her position and felt her stomach tighten.

"She is my sister," said Antelope Runner. "Kit Fox, what are you doing?"

"Nothing," she squeaked. And then she repeated to herself, nothing, more firmly. Turning in a fast circle, she handed the reins to Found Arrow and gave him a glance safe from the others' eyes. She strode past them to pick up her bow and quiver. "I brought my bow out, then thought I would see if the guard was riding the horse yet."

Raven stepped forward to twitch the reins from Found Arrow's hand. "Get down. Who said you could mount him?"

"I said Found Arrow could try," observed Chief Kills Bear. "You young warriors always do what you want, anyway. I am more concerned about the young woman. This is the second time I have met you here, Kit Fox. Tell me what you were doing."

Kit Fox lowered her eyes modestly, knowing she could not hide her blush. "I tried to ride the horse, too. My grandmother knows I am here."

"Not as bad. But does she know you came alone?"

"No."

"Go back to camp immediately." The war chief turned to Found Arrow, dismissing the girl. "Do not get down. Can you make that beast run?"

Found Arrow leaned forward on the horse's neck and looked toward his friend, Kit Fox. "I can race him. And I think he might permit Kit Fox to ride him as well."

"This is a matter for warriors," Kills Bear roared. "At last the council have agreed so. At last! But only after Star Child and Cuts Buffalo have died at the hands of the Snakes because the Snakes had horses and our warriors did not!"

They were the last words Kit Fox heard as she scurried back down the trail, humiliated but too angry for tears. But she knew she would be back. For the first time ever in her life she thought that maybe Old Holy Woman was right when she shook her gray locks and said, "Men!"

The sight of her little brother, Cub, raised her spirits. Tomorrow the march to the summer camp would begin. She would not have been able to ride the horse again until they reached there. Before then she would have Old Holy Woman's help. Meanwhile, she thought, she had a younger brother dancing across the grass to meet her.

"So your friend Calf is better?" asked Kit Fox.

"Yes. She will come on the march with us, tied to a travois. She is healing." Cub tugged at the buckskin fringe on his sister's sleeve. "Come, come see our new kettle!"

Kit Fox could not believe her eyes. Their new kettle was bigger than anyone else's—twice the size of a local clay pot. It even had a copper lid. Everyone wanted to see this new thing Whiteweasel had bought from the Assiniboin, who had bought it from the Hudson's Bay Company.

But on first sight Old Holy Woman was inclined to sell it to some other family, right away. "How will we carry that monster the distance between camps? Not on my back."

Whiteweasel hefted its shiny copper belly over his head to show how light it was.

"You may lift it, Whiteweasel," the old lady said, "but it would take a two-dog travois to haul it—and you know what kind of riot that means."

"Mother, any dog with a bit of wolf in him could haul this kettle. Our dogs are strong. Remember, one of them hauls all eight skins of our tipi cover. This kettle is so light, it is only good exercise for a mutt. Even Cub could lift it."

He smiled and rubbed his finger over Cub's forehead as the little boy grinned up at him. At a nod from his father, Cub slid his arms under the arc of the handle and jerked them upward. He walked two steps, grunting in concentration, the kettle banging against the curve of his stomach with each step. There was a surprised look on his face when he dropped it. His father grabbed the edge just in time to prevent damage to Cub's toes.

Cub laughed. Kit Fox thought, he knows he is pleasing.

Friends from neighboring tipis gathered. Most of the women stroked the kettle admiringly, while the men stood back and joked about it. Kit Fox heard one old lady murmur that the old ways were always better. Her son's wife nodded doubtfully, then turned to Three Catcher and asked how she meant to cook in that copper monster. So much more kettle to clean!

Kit Fox shuffled backward through the crowd, trying to

avoid that conversation. At a mother's request, she scooted around her to sooth a tearful baby hanging from her back in his cradleboard. She offered the child a taste of her finger.

A voice hissed from a person she could not see. "What a kettle! Do Whiteweasel and Three Catcher not think the old ways fine enough for their family?"

An elderly lady to Kit Fox's right hitched up her robe against the freezing wind, as she answered Took Two Lance. "Perhaps the kettle was meant for a present to a certain young man's parents."

Kit Fox thought, which young man? Could it be Raven Tail Feathers? If so, then the time for Many Deer to go to his tipi must be near. Many Deer could not like the idea, Kit thought, but if the ceremonies of gift-giving stopped these nasty jealousies then that would be good.

The baby drooled over her thumb. She pulled it out of his mouth, dried it on the cradleboard cover and patted him on his cheek. It was time to leave.

She found Swift Hands Woman chirping cheerfully about how the new copper kettle was such a fine thing, and how glad she was to see these interesting novelties, "before I lie down in peace on the prairie, and you children go on without me."

"Nonsense—" Kit Fox began. The fragile old lady could not be serious. "We will make a good travois for you for the march."

A giant CLANG! interrupted her. Cub had not, after all, been content to prove that he could carry the heavy kettle. Someone had questioned whether the dog could carry it. Very well. He had carried it to the dog, and placed the kettle over the dog's head.

The inside of the kettle echoed from the endless barking. Finally the poor dog tried to back out of the situation, shaking his head as he sidled backward.

"Bad, bad child!" his mother scolded Cub, between gusts of laughter.

Kit Fox laughed until she could taste the salt of her tears.

CHAPTER NINE

Many Deer's cheeks were rosy with excitement, and her eyes bright as the sun just peeking over the horizon. "This morning we march!"

"Land rich with game again," Kit Fox said, with enthusiasm. "We have eaten almost everything around here."

Many Deer agreed. "Raven Tail Feathers says this year's summer campsite in the Eagle Hills has porcupines, beaver dams and a place where you can dig the sacred red clay. Green algae in the lake—"

"Scummy for swimming!"

"But excellent for dyeing porcupine quills green. We are almost out of quills, you know. I am so happy they chose the Eagle Hills! Do you think Cub is old enough to learn to get porcupines by rolling them over with a stick?"

"He will come out of the woods looking like the largest porcupine you have ever seen," answered Kit Fox, looking around to see where their next-to-youngest brother had gone. Perhaps he was making a nuisance of himself in one of the tipis that had not yet been taken down.

"No, he will not," said Many Deer, then, following a moment's thought, "after the first two or three times."

And there was Cub's face, glaring at them from behind a neighbor's travois. He raised himself further and loosed an imaginary arrow in their direction. Then he sank again, down into his hiding place to be concealed for the next ambush.

Many Deer ducked, her arm over her head, as if to ward off an imaginary blow.

The girls poked each other with their elbows and giggled. They saw their grandmother and her co-wife watching them from the packed travois on which they sat along with the baby still on his cradleboard. The women waited for Three Catcher's return with the last reluctant dog.

"What are you girls giggling about?" yelled Old Holy Woman.

Swift Hands Woman leaned forward, petting her hand and twittering, "We are so glad to see you happy. Are we not, my sister?"

"Why would we be?"

The girls wondered who in the camp overheard this. Even softened, Old Holy Woman's voice had significant carrying power. Swift Hands Woman nudged her.

"Very well, giggling is better than sullen, if there is no further choice," the fat co-wife muttered. The girls knew that she really loved them, if not as much as she loved the other old lady with whom she had so long shared a tipi. She continued, "But if our husband were alive, he would take my side."

"Hi-yah, she is still a warrior woman," Swift Hands Woman pronounced, and giggled, showing off the pink of her long gums and the black gap where she had lost two of her teeth.

Many Deer grinned politely. As the old women lost interest in them, she pulled her sister around so their backs were to the camp and they could be private. "Anyhow, Raven Tail Feathers says that the new campsite is thickly wooded, with aspen for safe firewood, and evergreens."

"Fur and spruce trees for sparkly fires, outside the tipi where sparks are safe—"

"Great dances and storytelling in the nighttime!" agreed Many Deer. "In the woods there will be deer. We can make more white buckskin."

Kit Fox gasped. "More? But we have—"

"We had only one hide, and I have used part of it." Many Deer's cheeks glowed. "I cut out a special pair of moccasins yesterday. Mother and Father told me the husband they prefer for me, and I agreed with them. His parents agree, too. Will you help me with the quillwork for my dress?"

Who could refuse Many Deer's pleading eyes, framed with lashes thick as mink fur? Kit Fox asked, "It is Raven Tail Feathers, is it not?"

"Yes. Or Raven Pinfeathers, if you listen to Old Holy Woman. Why, do you still mind?"

Kit Fox managed to yawn. She said, "I am so tired from getting up early for the final packing and taking

102

down the tipi. No, I do not mind. Marry him if you are sure he is worthy of you, and if you love him."

She hoped Many Deer accepted her thoughts on this, too, and they did not have to have bad words between them.

Their mother arrived. She hauled a big, wolfish, cream and black dog with her. He snapped as she harnessed him to the heavily loaded travois. "Bad!" she scolded. "We will have to keep an eye on you on the march, you wicked coyote. Now, you, Many Deer, help me make Swift Hands Woman comfortable on the two-dog travois."

The old lady tittered. "If it is possible for anyone to be comfortable on a two-dog travois. I am afraid they will start a fight when we are out on the flat prairie. This wolf-creature will run off with half my old bones in one direction, and that wolf-creature with the other half in the other direction."

"Here, put your hand on my arm," offered Many Deer.

"It will be the only thing that has ever happened to me worse than my aching joints," Swift Hands Woman continued. "He wants to eat me alive. Can you not smell the hunger on him?"

"Nonsense!" stated Three Catcher. She pushed them along with one firm hand behind the wing of the old lady's fragile shoulderbone. "I fed the dogs on buffalo bones this very morning. Sit down on that travois. We will strap you in—"

"So I cannot fall out," a tired and resigned voice grumbled.

The march began in early morning and went until the

sun reached its peak in the sky when they halted for a cold meal. Almost everyone was walking. Dog travois were only for the toddlers or the very sick. Kit Fox's band would need seven more days to finish the journey. A war party could have run the distance in three. But a war party would not have been carrying the entire camp on dog travois or on their shoulders.

Kit Fox was glad of the call to rest as she unfastened the cradleboard of her newest brother from her back. All around her, people were laying down their burdens: weapons, packs and babies.

She munched her portion of dried meat quickly. Where was Many Deer? Not Song Sparrow or anyone could tell her where Many Deer was in the procession that straggled down the trail and wound through the shoulder-high grass of the prairie as the march began again.

Heat waves shimmered under the featureless blue bowl of the sky. Even if you stood on someone's shoulders, Kit Fox thought, you would see nothing but prairie and more prairie, flat on all sides of you. She disentangled the baby's fingers from a strand of her hair. Her back sagged beneath the weight of cradleboard and growing baby. Her feet ached.

The long, line of people had passed the fork where the Red Deer River joined the South Saskatchewan River and now swung north across open prairie. Kit Fox knew Found Arrow would be leading Eagle Flies Over Hills, somewhere near the front of the line, out of range of her vision. She wished she were there to help her friend control the animal. She wished she could ride today. When they had many horses . . . Her mind drifted into its favorite daydream.

Then without warning her sister's voice sank into her back like a cold stone knife. "So why do you hate Raven, Kit Fox?"

"Many Deer!" Kit Fox spun on her heel. "I do not hate Raven. I just do not like him. Most of the time," she added, remembering when he had lent her his snake-skin bow. But still, she could not forget his actions with the horse. Raven had a dark side and she feared it. She feared it for her sister as well.

"Took Two Lance just told me you like his brother well enough, that you were spending every morning with Found Arrow and the horse! Is it true?"

Never before had Kit Fox seen such an expression on Many Deer's face. Kit Fox asked, angered, "What is wrong with it?"

"You—alone with him!"

"It was the horse I went to visit, not Found Arrow. Grandmother knows. She is helping me follow a vision I had of riding the horse."

Her sister now looked thoughtful.

Kit Fox continued, "You know Old Holy Woman says Took Two Lance has a snake in her belly. Why would you listen to her?"

"Yes. She is a jealous, mean, troublemaking person, sometimes," Many Deer agreed without hesitation. "She warps what she sees. But that does not mean what she sees is always false."

"Aiii. Everyone is jealous sometimes. Sometimes I am even jealous of you and Raven," Kit Fox admitted with a sigh. "But I still like Found Arrow better than his brother. Come now, we have to rejoin the march." Kit Fox put up a hand to check the cradleboard's balance.

"This baby adds as much weight as if I were pregnant," she complained. "My feet ache."

"If you were pregnant, the weight would be on your front and it would be your back that would ache," commented Many Deer. She swung into her stride again.

"Right now I think maybe that would feel better." Kit Fox bent all her tact and sense of humor to avoiding a quarrel.

But the lines of anger were forming around Many Deer's mouth again. "How can you not like Raven, when I love him? We always used to think the same. How can you be so stubborn?"

Kit Fox blurted out, "You will like Raven until the first day he hurts you." Kit Fox did not want to upset her sister, but she could not help her feelings against Raven.

Why did her sister have to insist Kit Fox feel the way she herself did? She tried to leave. She wanted to get away before she said anything more Many Deer could not bear to hear, anything more for which her sister would not forgive her. The baby flopped against his cradleboard as it shifted against Kit Fox's back. Up and down, up and down. Dust and pollen from the grassheads was crusted inside her nostrils.

Many Deer panted at her side. "What a horrible thing to say, Kit Fox! Raven will never hurt me." Her eyes peered around the edge of the cradleboard. They were suddenly sly. "Raven will never hurt me—if you are my co-wife."

A cradleboard string was carving a welt just under Kit Fox's left shoulderblade. She stopped to pull at the front part of the strap. "My sister—hear me. You may choose

106

what you wish. Whatever your choice, you know I love you." She saw that the sly look was gone from Many Deer's face and her sister was really listening now. Kit Fox knew she had never spoken this way to anyone before. Could she have, before that last talk with Found Arrow? "I have listened to you with an open heart. Please love me and hear me. Now I must choose my own path."

Many Deer lowered her head with a brooding look. Kit Fox gently offered another distraction. When a toad jumped in the high grass, she leapt to grab him. "Oooo—his skin—I would rather hold a leech. Why not take him to Calf's travois? She must be bored."

"Kit Fox!"

"We can talk about the men later, if you really want. They are only men, after all, not anything for sisters to fight over. Think instead of pitiful little Calf. Would you want to be jolted along, tied to a travois?"

Many Deer managed half a smile. "She is lucky to be light enough to be tied to a dog-travois. What if we had to leave her? And after she got well she and her mother had to try to catch up?"

"If she was not eaten first by bears or wolves or wolverines—" said Kit Fox.

"If she was not knifed first by Flatheads or Kootenais or Snakes—"

They chanted together, making up the words between them as they went: "frozen by Old Man Frost, shivered by the coughing-sickness, withered by starvation—"

"What would happen to us if we were not brave?" asked Many Deer, suddenly.

They jogged again, breasting the long grasses with their arms, until they sighted Calf's travois. "Here is a toad, Calf."

"My dog wants to eat him."

Kit Fox pushed the dog's nose away and warned him to keep his travois in motion.

"Here," she offered Calf, trying to make her voice tempting, "you can hold the pretty toad." Kit Fox was pleased to see Calf's strength returning. She held out her hand.

"You will have to hold him or he will jump," Kit Fox warned as she set the toad down, but—too late. Once it sensed freedom, it hopped for the high grass and the dog bounded after it.

"Grab his harness!" shouted Many Deer.

Two boys raced by, waving their arms and kiyaaing. So far Calf's dog had run parallel to the trail. Kit Fox could see the travois ahead of them was also jolting along. She heard the yaps mixed with shrieks and growls from the other dogs.

"Dog fight!" Calf cried.

"Dog fight and runaway dog travois," shouted Five Killer between heavy breaths, as he passed them. He held his lance close to his side. He added, "Baby in travois . . ." Soon he was out of their sight.

Calf's dog shied from the weapon. Many Deer and Kit Fox jumped him, from opposite ends. Wonder of wonders, the baby in his cradleboard on her back continued to sleep. They all collapsed by the travois, Kit Fox draped over the panting mutt. "That is right, pant with your tongue so far out that you eat dirt," she advised

108

him. "We made certain this dog travois did not run away," she called to Old Holy Woman.

Her grandmother puffed and waddled to them. "The heat! The dust! The vultures!" she exclaimed as she plumped down.

"What vultures? There are no vultures."

"Do you not see vultures overhead? They have been following us across the plains all day, waiting for me," replied Old Holy Woman.

"Better vultures than Snakes," ventured Many Deer. They all were silent for a while after that. Finally she asked, "How is it with Swift Hands Woman?"

The other old lady shook her head. "She is the last one in the line. Two-dog travois never work—keeping one dog on the trail is enough to wear out a woman's tongue and patience. She seems so frail these times that everything hurts. And she keeps telling me she would rather walk."

Kit Fox felt her love well up, a prickly ball in her throat. She said, slowly, so she could control the need to cry, "But she cannot walk."

Hands clutching the round ball of her belly as if it were a child with whom she was pregnant, Old Holy Woman sat unspeaking. Then she sighed. She rocked as if trying to comfort herself. "Thirty-five years we have lived in the same tipi. I know her, I know almost every gesture she makes before she makes it. But this I cannot understand."

She raised her eyebrows and said in a choked voice, "I do not think she wants to walk. She says this is the last march she will ever make. She says next time she wants to stay behind."

CHAPTER TEN

The deer walked delicate and silent as ghosts in the cool gray mist of deep forest's morning. A fawn, a yearling and a doe, their narrow hooves paced heedlessly down the mossy trail to the bog to drink. Kit Fox waited with her arrow on the string.

She sighted over the yearling, then brought her bow down and released. She knew as the string resonated under her hand that her aim was true. But from nowhere a violent wind blasted through the fog, driving the poplars to slash at each other, the hair to stand up along the backs of the deer, and Kit Fox's arrow to land wide. The deer shivered, then ran.

The wind disappeared. Kit Fox shook herself with wonder, but it was true. Before the final flicker of deer tails down the path, mist hovered again in the air, eerily still.

Her spine turned to an icicle. She had dreamed this, the night before, warm in her bed at the band's summer camp. In her dream, though, it had been a rabbit at which she aimed, with an arrow she watched fly true. Just as the arrow touched the rabbit's breast, a great gray owl swooped and caught the shaft in her beak. Her wings beat downward once, hiding the arrow from the dreamer's sight. They rose in their upward beat—and the arrow was gone. There the dream ended.

Kit Fox shivered, remembering, alone in the damp dawn. What did it mean? Was it a bad omen? She stumbled through underbrush toward the growing light, forcing saplings back from her path until she found the clearing. Low prairie roses bent, white smudges, under her moccasins. She hurried toward the comfort of the camp.

If only she could ride the horse, that would give her comfort. But she could not. Found Arrow had been gone for two days now on his vision quest, and someone else had taken his place guarding Eagle Flies Over Hills. Kit Fox wondered if she dared make a visit to the horse meadow.

She forced a smile to her face for the children, playing close to home in the clearing.

"I am a mighty hunter, see the hides of my prey?" Cub demanded, insisting she give him her attention.

"His name is not Cub anymore, it is Chewing Wolf Bones, and he is my husband," added the small girl with him. Kit Fox remembered that her name was Flute. Flute's smile was bounded by two very round, red cheeks.

Cub grabbed his sister's hand to drag her down nearer the toys they had spread over the grass. "See, Kit Fox? The eleven buffalo I caught?"

Wood splinters held several miniature hides pegged out

to dry against the ground. Others, already tanned, served now for toy tipi covers, furniture, or—stuffed with dried grass—their dogs. "Excellent," Kit Fox observed. To the little girl she commented, "The wife of such a mighty hunter must also work very hard."

"Yes," she agreed solemnly. "Today I made the last of the things we need, three travois for our dogs to pull. Swift Hands Woman showed me how." The travois poles were twigs, the harnesses of braided grass. "If my husband, the mighty hunter, brings home more gophers today, I say he must be generous and give them to the unlucky, the kimataps. We have all the dried meat we need and as much else as our dogs can carry."

Kit Fox had to hide her face against the fringe of her sleeve to keep from laughter. Flute's pursed lips so resembled the look Flute's mother gave her father under those circumstances.

Cub swung one of the gopher travois up beside a white-haired doll figure. "Old lady, on my travois is half a buffalo. I, Chewing Wolf Bones, make you a present of this."

Kit Fox joined the game, speaking in a cracked old voice. "It is good. Chewing Wolf Bones, you are indeed a mighty hunter, a wise man and generous."

The children burst into laughter. Cub explained, "Kit Fox, you have a funny voice."

Three Catcher was inside the tipi, as her daughter expected. She was working busily, also as expected, punching holes along the edge of a hide with her long, wickedly pointed awl. "At last, Kit Fox. Help me with this new tipi cover. You did not wander out of camp alone, did you, so early in the morning?"

"Do you want me to start sewing the hides together? Are we using the deer sinew? There are only a few lengths left, you know. I hoped to get you some more this morning, but . . . luck was not with my shooting." Kit Fox knelt and, placing the sinew thread in her mouth, began to soften it. She noticed her mother had not replied. Three Catcher had put down her awl.

Three Catcher rubbed absent-mindedly along one foot, down the edge of the sole, around the heel, along the edge to the moccasin tip. Her hand paused.

Kit Fox noticed that her mother's brow was drawn into three long wrinkles across its width. She took the thread from her mouth and asked, "Mother? Are you well?"

"Aiii, child! I hate to speak of it," said Three Catcher.

"Tell me."

"I—" She drew a deep breath, then ventured, her voice expressionless, "I heard the owl in the nighttime."

The owl's cry often warned of a coming death. Kit Fox shut her eyes. "Mother, I think I did, too. More than that—"

Kit Fox shared the details of her dream, and how it had repeated itself when she loosed her arrow at the deer. And Kit Fox knew that to miss a sure shot also often was a sign of a coming death.

Three Catcher gently removed the sinew thread from her hands. "Daughter, perhaps you should go now and visit little Calf. I have heard no news for several days."

The healer woman was bent over Calf when Kit Fox arrived. The girl was happy to hear that Calf's voice, at least, sounded more than healthy enough. "No, no, no," she was squeaking, "I will not drink it."

The healer woman smiled at the visitor, but Kit Fox

guessed from the length of the lines running down her cheeks that she was weary to the marrow of her bones. In her hands she held a wooden bowl. She said, "It is a tea—willow bark and the plant the Cree call museko-pukwa. I used too much of the museko-pukwa for her delicate stomach last time. Now she will not drink it."

"I vomited over everything!" Calf could not wait to tell Kit Fox.

"But this time I have made it just the right strength for you, and you will not vomit," the older woman explained. "The medicine tea will put out the fire in your body. Then you will have more strength to become well. Smell it—does it not smell delicious?"

From the bowl wafted the scent of licorice. "Aksowa root," the healer noted, for Kit Fox's benefit. She knew Kit Fox was a young person interested in herbal medicine.

"I know it. Old Holy Woman taught me. These herbs together are what Calf needs to feel better?"

"So she can sleep, poor pitiful buffalo calf." The child looked up, convinced at last.

When the small body curled limp on its sleeping couch, Kit Fox whispered to the healer: would the child really be better soon? The answer cheered her. Calf grew steadily stronger, and her friends need not worry for her. Kit Fox sighed. It must be that she and her mother had been concerned without reason, since no one close to their family except Calf was ill.

That night, as she lay wrapped and close to sleep in her warm sleeping robes, she called the image of Found Arrow into her mind. As she imagined being with him

114

and Eagle Flies Over Hills, she smiled. If only she could visit the horse. All she could think about was how much she wanted to see him again. As she fell asleep, she prayed for a chance, a reason to go to the horse meadow. Did she dare risk it? If Chief Kills Bear with Knife spoke to her father, Kit Fox might be severely punished.

She had been right, of course. The next morning at the horse meadows the guard on duty, a grizzled old warrior she had known since she was Cub's size, hardly pretended to listen to her rattle on about the horse.

There was no use trying to explain.

"Pat him, then, child, but do not come back again to feed him." The guard's voice was gruff, though Kit Fox knew he did not mean to be unkind. He added, "And run back to your mother now, quickly."

Kit Fox stroked the rich, dark fur. The horse seemed to remember her; he did not pull away. She gave Eagle Flies Over Hills one last pat on his soft nose. As she left the meadow, she heard his questioning nicker behind her. She could not wait for the day when she might ride him again.

She ran all the way to camp, looking for Many Deer, needing her sister's comfort. Many Deer's smile always brought the rainbow into her storms.

"Kit Fox," Many Deer greeted her, smiling a glad welcome. "We have something exciting to tell you."

Her friend Song Sparrow also smiled as she looked up. Her baby's mossbag was open on the grass, and she was cleaning his bottom with clean-scented sage leaves.

"Hello, Song Sparrow and baby. Baby, you do not remember me, but I watched you in your tent during last dance." Kit Fox ran a finger around one tiny ear, translucent as eggshell, and stroked the tufts of black hair. His mother lifted him by placing a hand under his neck and back, and tucked him into his mossbag. Kit Fox watched them as she asked, "Tell me your news."

Many Deer said, "Raven Tail Feathers' parents sent presents to our tipi—and Father and Mother accepted them. Now we must send presents in our turn. Everyone wishes us to marry!"

Kit Fox had never seen her so beautiful. So intense was Many Deer's happiness that Kit Fox could almost smell it. The lilt in her voice, the confident grace with which she tossed her braids back over her shoulder, her tender anticipation as she stroked Song Sparrow's baby. Who could say she was doing the wrong thing, if it made her so happy? What harm could there be in simply being happy for her?

"I am happy for your happiness," Kit Fox said slowly. She rubbed the red bump that had grown overnight on her chin. It had a painful core.

Despite her happy preoccupation, her sister noticed. "You should boil some leaves of wild bergamot," she advised, her tone suddenly practical. "If you place them on the bump, they will dry it."

Song Sparrow coughed to call their attention to the man approaching. Long, shiny black hair hung, tied with elk antler ornaments, over the stranger's broad shoulders.

"One of the Cree warriors," announced Song Sparrow. "Kills Bear with Knife greeted their trading party today. This one is good-looking. Do you agree, Kit Fox? I wonder if he needs a wife?"

Many Deer asked, tactfully, "Is it true that the Cree brought a new wonder with them?"

"True. A mystery in a long buckskin case, longer than any bowcase I ever saw," said Song Sparrow.

"What kind of a mystery?" asked Kit Fox.

"My husband's mother told me it was powerful medicine for us to use against the Snake tribe." Song Sparrow hugged her baby. "Something to protect you, joy of my life!"

Many Deer nodded her head. "Ah. A new weapon."

"This I wish to see," said Kit Fox.

"At the council meeting in two days," promised Song Sparrow. "But for now, there is nothing more to tell."

"I have gossip to tell you, also," Kit Fox said. "You remember our favorite friend, Took Two Lance?"

Song Sparrow laughed sarcastically.

"She is to be married."

The others stared. Kit Fox was glad to notice that even the baby stopped gurgling and stared with solemn, charcoal-black eyes. Kit Fox repeated, "Yes—married. To a Peigan, one of our distant cousins to the south. Her uncle told me."

Many Deer raised her eyes to the sky and released peals of giggles. Song Sparrow stuffed her fist into her mouth to try to hold back some of her merriment. It only made her laugh harder. Both of them were laughing like boys of four winters whose first practical joke has been successful. Many Deer gasped for breath and an end to her spasms. She rubbed the palms of her hands against her sides.

"At last, at last," she rejoiced, more calmly. "Now we

117

shall have peace in camp. She hates me, though I have never wished her anything but happiness."

"Now she may have it." Song Sparrow bent to kiss her baby on his fat mushroom of a nose.

"Now we all may be happy!" said Many Deer. "Kit Fox, do you suspect Old Holy Woman had something to do with this? She told me that something had to be done about Took Two Lance, that she was growing a giant snake in her belly."

"And the more she fed it the bigger it got, and the bigger it got the more it ate away at the inside of her. I do not understand that."

"Perhaps once she is married she will have time only to love and work and be happy," said Many Deer. "That is all I want."

As she fell to sleep that night, Kit Fox thought—love, work and be happy—is that what I want? I have always wanted to make everyone else happy, too, but what if I want different things from what they think will make them happy? It never was that way before. I hope it never is that way again. Why does Many Deer have to want to marry Raven? Drowsily, eyes shut, she outlined the shape of the good luck butterfly against her sleeping robe. Then she relaxed her arms and let her thoughts follow the winding river of melody flowing from Raven Tail Feathers' flute. The music moved her heart.

He must really care for Many Deer, she thought with wonder, if he keeps coming to play his flute at night outside her tipi even after she has agreed to marry him. Usually men only court women until the women accept. Her buffalo robe enclosed her in darkness. She faded into sleep and dreamed her powerful dream.

Next morning she described the dream to her father, seeking its meaning, if it proved a true vision.

"The cougar's eyes lanced me with fire. I could not look away, I stretched my neck up, offered my throat. He did not lean down. But one paw dragged the bridle in the horse's mouth until blood ran red along the reins. The horse's hooves drummed against the earth as the cougar held him, motionless there. I trembled. I was filled with awe, because he had chosen to come to me.

"I heard the torch crackle as he lifted it high over-head. And the smell of it as it burned was something I never smelled before, worse than stinkwood, worse than rotting flesh. A smell to make vomit rise in your throat.

"But the cougar's eyes—Aiii, my father! I wish that I could dream it again, all for seeing the glory of the cougar's sunset eyes.

"What does this mean, this vision that my shadow saw while my body was sleeping?" she continued.

There was a long silence. Then Kit Fox's father slowly shook his head. He looked into her eyes, his own filled with compassion, and said, "I do not know. But your grandmother was right to send you to me. This is a message for the band. Tomorrow I will tell the council."

CHAPTER ELEVEN

There, under the cranberry bush, her snare dangled a weasel. Three Catcher would not be impressed with this as a gift for the stewpot. But the glossy brown fur had much value. Maybe she would make it into a present for her friend to tie in his hair.

Overhead the forest leaves trembled in a light breeze, and she shivered. Tonight, her father would tell her dream to the council. Being up here reminded her again of Found Arrow, because he had said he would go to one of these lonelier heights of the Eagle Hills to seek his spiritual helper. She had not ridden the horse for the four days her friend had been away.

Many men returned, successful, from wilderness fasting and prayer for a spiritual helper in less time than four days. They returned with tales of power given them by their helper, with dances, medicine bundles, tipi designs, ceremonies or songs. In this way whichever symbols they received of their sacred medicine could always be with them. The medicine would aid them in hunting, war or other assistance to their people.

Some men never came back at all.

Kit Fox shook her head to drive away the fears. Found Arrow did not need her worrying; he had done all the elders suggested. Surely he would be rewarded. All he needed was her prayers.

She pulled cranberries into her hand, sampling their acid taste. She decided to follow the watercourse along the ravine. Where there were puddles of water, there should be game.

Silverweed grew in mats over the muddy slopes, tied by surface runners. The delicate, ferny green sprigs with their yellow flowers spread in mad irregular leaps, like strawberries. The girl tugged strings of runners and rip-roots from the mud as she trotted down the shortcut of the ravine bottom. Brewed, the roots would ease chest pains.

A jumble of animal tracks pressed into the mud confirmed the range of creatures that came here to the pond to drink. Kit Fox immediately spotted tracks of dogs, giant elk and a white-tailed deer. Were those moccasin prints, along the path at the pond's opposite edge?

Yes. And over them, at the end in the direction of the sunset, were pressed the round prints of a massive cougar.

She followed their trail. Farther back from the pond the moon-shaped tracks of deer overlapped those of the cougar. Kit Fox never doubted the order of the visits: first came the man and the dog; then the cougar; last the deer. The deer had been here last night or this morning. Whenever it was, it would only be after the cougar scent had disappeared. Kit Fox remembered the thunderstorm of the night before last night, and its torrents of rain beating flat the grass and the tracks pressed into the ground. So all tracks here were younger than that.

She traced the cougar further, to where the prints of his furred pads wiped out the moccasin prints of the man. The man's trail curved back there, to a clump of yellow birch trees, more fragile than the surrounding spruce and aspens of the forest, and a boulder. On the boulder rested a curl of birchbark. A pebble held it flat.

Kit Fox raced across the clearing. It must be a message such as the warriors and hunters of her people often left for whoever crossed their trails. She could not believe it, but it seemed to be by the hand of Found Arrow. He must have hoped someone would pass this way and carry his news home to his friends and family at the nearby camp.

He had first traced his own pictograph: an arrow grasped by the five fingers of a hand. Beside this crouched the figure of a cougar. Another arrow pointed to the southwest. That was all he had written. No pictographs recording war deeds done or other prey killed. Nor did he record any vision.

The girl sighed. At least now she knew he had got this far. And she knew he had shot the cougar and then headed farther up into the hills to the southwest.

Her gaze slipped back to the cougar's prints. They did not surprise her: had she not seen a cougar in her dream? She wondered if the dream had been an omen of this cougar tracking Found Arrow.

* * *

Whiteweasel said, "So, my brothers, the smoke from the torch stank like death, like an egg that has gone rotten in the nest. Cougar did not even sniff at the smell. He sat on the horse's back, looking down at the dreamer, and by his side he held the flaming stick.

"Hear me. The girl says that she saw this, and that she has told us all, and that this is the truth. Now judge the meaning."

Whiteweasel returned to his place in the center ring of the evening's open air circle. Then the sounds of heated discussion, disbelief, wonderment, expressed in eight or ten conversations, rose above the council fire. But Whiteweasel did not join in this. Kit Fox held back in the shadows, observing the gathering.

Kills Bear with Knife was the next to rise to his feet. He said he thought Kit Fox's dream had to do with what the next speaker would say. Then he introduced the visiting representatives of their allies, the Cree. A Cree leader waved his long, mysterious buckskin case in the air as he began his speech.

"Bloods and Cree go to war together as allies," he said. "Now we are friends. Of course, it has not always been so. Even as the Snake people once were your friends, and now are your enemies, and may come to be your friends again. The napikwan people come in herds from the south and the east," he said. "Maybe one day we will all have to be friends if we are to have allies against them. But now we, the Cree, trade with both the napikwan and you. Many of the mighty warriors I see here, my people have faced in battle.

"Look, here on my arm, here is a scar from the knife of Whiteweasel, who has just spoken. My own brother once counted coup against Kills Bear with Knife," stated the Cree chief.

At this, Chief Kills Bear with Knife nodded. He fingered the bear claws on his necklace. From his smile, Kit Fox guessed that old stories crowded to his memory. But he let only a grunt of agreement escape him.

The buckskin case in the hand of their ally swung in front of them like a lance, but from the way he hefted it, it was some heavier weapon. Casually, he raised it over his head. The man nearest leaned back, startled. Again, conversation buzzed. This Cree chief had the instincts of a true performer.

"We come with aid for you, our allies. You Bloods need to move against your enemy, the Snake people. They are our enemies also. They own many horses. They ride north into our territories, and the Cree have no horses yet. So we cannot ride against them. But the Crees and the Cutthroats possess another weapon, something we got from the napikwan traders. Now I will show you this new weapon of great power. Here is—a weapon that makes thunder—"

He slipped a rod from its case like a snake from its loose skin. But what he held in his hand was something they had never seen before. Kit Fox heard her own breath rattle in her throat, fast and shallow in her excitement. Everyone stared at the weapon. The assembly buzzed like a giant hive again. Only Kills Bear with Knife remained impassive. Of course, she thought, he has seen these new weapons before. He had gone with the Assiniboin to the Hudson's Bay Company napikwan traders.

"I think that weapon is made of something like our copper kettle," Many Deer whispered in Kit Fox's ear. "Except the color is different—not copper, but silver like an old lady's hair."

"No one is to stand up!" the Cree chief ordered. He waved his hand at the rows of people sitting on the earth before him. "No one! I will make it speak thunder over your heads."

From a pouch he poured powder down the mouth of the flintlock. From a second pouch he produced a round metal berry. He dropped this also into the gun's muzzle.

"What was that?" whispered Many Deer. She wrapped her fingers around a stone, black-speckled on a buff ground and shaped like a plover's egg, which she wore around her neck on a thong. Kit Fox could only shrug. She knew they would all learn what it was, and quickly.

Next the Cree chief aimed along the length of his weapon. If that were a bow and arrow I would say he holds his position too long, thought Kit Fox. She counted her heartbeats, waiting.

Then he fired, and the air split inside her skull. She saw the mouth of the weapon spout flame. Out in the darkness a sapling split with a crack. Sulfur fumes wafted their rotten smell through the air. She grabbed Many Deer, who was keening and holding both hands to her ears.

A child raced screaming around the dark rim of the assembly. His mother stumbled after, but no one caught him. The council itself was in uproar.

In their center, the Cree chief calmly stood, cleaning the mouth of his flintlock. Now Kit Fox knew why he said thunder lived in it.

She heard a voice recounting her own dream of cougar, riding triumphant on his horse, his evil-smelling torch in hand. Late into the night the council debated the wisest action for this time. Their decision was to use the Cree offer of the guns and strike for the Snake raiding parties. They all hoped security would come from this war.

Kit Fox sat on the floor of her parents' tipi with her bow across her knees. She chewed the inside of her lip thoughtfully. Found Arrow still had not come back. Now she had true reason for worry. Her cougar dream was an omen of the coming of the gun, not some harm to him, she hoped.

She knew she had courage for action, but it was harder, sometimes, to have the courage, strength and endurance to leave others their own right of action and wait. Had anyone noticed her worry? No. She bent to her work again.

Old Holy Woman was asking a question of her father. "Do you not think you are old for this, Morning Bird?"

"Many summers have passed since you last called me by my childhood name," said Whiteweasel. From his tone of voice his daughter guessed his mind was elsewhere, too. His hands greased the sinew of his war bow, up and down, as disinterestedly as if it was only a chore.

Old Holy Woman and Three Catcher worked busily, sewing together the pieces of the new tipi cover. Kit Fox had decided to take advantage of her father's bear grease to grease her own bow. From where she sat by a birch sapling, she watched the ferocity of her mother's attack on the tipi cover. Grandmother, too, thrust the sinew through the holes in the hide as if she were instead destroying an enemy.

His job finished, Whiteweasel stretched his back. Next he bent over Three Catcher. He rested one hand on the nape of his wife's neck. He laced his fingers through the raven-black hair that fell to her waist.

"Will you sew extra moccasins for me, for the war trail?" he asked Old Holy Woman, still standing with his hand twined in his wife's hair.

"It is already done."

"Good. You sew fine moccasins, old lady," said Whiteweasel, affectionately.

Between mother and son there passed a look of tenderness. It did not need to last long, Kit Fox knew, because it was only a reminder of what both held inside. No quarrel could change that.

Whiteweasel ran a finger over Cub's forehead as he passed the wolfpack of children gathered around the spinning-tops. He stooped to show his next-to-youngest how best to flick the top with his willow wand for a long spin. Then he was gone.

Old Holy Woman held her hand over her eyes as if the brightness of the sunlight made it hard for her to see her sewing. She asked Three Catcher, "Where are Antelope Runner and Bad Eyes?"

"At the sweat lodge, making themselves ready for the war trail," she said softly, then called to Kit Fox, "Have you fed the dogs yet?"

As she hurried on her task she heard Old Holy Woman grumbling behind her. "Mutts. Good-for-nothing wolf dogs. Lazy creatures, always biting each other and getting into fights."

Kit Fox anticipated the look of gratitude her own yellow dog would give her when she put food before him. She knew her grandmother was not serious. She thought, I love dogs. And the horse. And some people, too.

Three Catcher sliced the calves of her legs with the stone knife clutched in her hand. She cut herself over and over. The blood streamed from a dozen gashes. Tears flowed down her breast and cheeks. Alone she wailed as she stood in her blood on the hilltop. Around her the Eagle Hills throbbed with the tears of the women, each hearing the others, each alone in her own space with grief.

They keened for their dead. Their black hair blew, unbraided and untended, in the rain and the wind.

It had been a great victory.

Nevertheless, the women slashed themselves, they fasted, they wailed and they bled. One cut herself so deeply in her pain that she fainted. But nothing could bring back her husband-to-be. For fifteen days he had been gone from her sight, and then the war party returned with the news that she would never see him again.

When the time for mourning was finished, Three Catcher painted her moccasins black with charcoal in memory of her oldest son. Then she returned to her life. She tended the old ladies, she lay awake long hours sharing hopes and problems with her husband. But of one thing she and Whiteweasel did not speak.

Finally, ten days after the war party's return, Three Catcher asked her younger daughter. "I could not listen when your father and Bad Eyes returned. Tell me now. What is the story of Antelope Runner's last war deeds?"

Kit Fox turned her gaze to the man who was now her oldest brother. "Bad Eyes? Can you tell her?"

"Hi-yah. Listen then, and I will tell you." Bad Eyes breathed deeply and began his story.

"For six days we walked south. It was good traveling. Many buffalo. Our scout found a Snake camp on the seventh morning. That was Antelope Runner who found it and let us know. Because of his sharp eyes, he was a good scout."

Three Catcher mumbled something, but she shook her head when her children asked her to repeat it.

Bad Eyes continued, "We had stopped to eat, when we saw him near the top of one of those buttes that rise out of the prairie. He was just a speck of blackness at that distance. We knew he must have found something.

"He took off his buffalo robe and waved it. You know how warriors do that to send a message, Mother." Bad Eyes stood and, drawing off his own robe, whirled it around his head. "Ah! We knew he had the enemy sighted.

"Kills Bear with Knife cried out, 'He whirls the robe slowly. That means the enemy's camp is far away!' Then it was as if Antelope Runner changed his mind. He began waving his robe like this," and Bad Eyes whirled the robe in a quick, tight circle. "We all wondered—what did it mean? Were the enemy far away, or were they near?

129

"The Snake people were camped far away, but they had sent out a war party on horseback. That is why Antelope Runner signaled both that they were close and that they were far away. They advanced on us faster than anyone could have thought possible. By the time Antelope Runner signaled, the Snakes were already on the other side of the butte. They reached us before he could make his way back.

"At Antelope Runner's signal, we started to paint ourselves for battle, thinking we had time. But they took us by surprise. There were ten Snake warriors on horseback. There were seventeen of us on foot. Father and the other archers strung their bows at the first sight of them, and took up their positions under the cover of a low ravine.

"I crept through the long grass to a silverberry bush not far from their path. Because the Snakes were on horseback they looked down on us. How can men on foot in the grass hide from men on horseback? But me, hidden from their eyes by the branches around me, they somehow did not see.

"Kills Bear with Knife asked the Cree to lie, as hidden as they could, in the ravine with the guns. The weapons that speak thunder were to be our surprise!

"The Snakes rode just short of arrow range from the ravine. Then they charged. I shot at them from behind—that was something they were not expecting. In an instant one of the Snakes rode back to stop me. The first time I put an arrow into the shoulder of his pony. But that Snake was stubborn and headed for me again. I thought, I will hold my arrow until he is near, then shoot before he can strike with his stone club for my head.

"And I did. But I do not know if that would have killed him or he would have killed me, because a lance skewered him and he fell to the ground. That was the first time I knew that Antelope Runner had come down from the butte. The Snake's body crumpled. I jumped and counted coup on him. Slit his throat, after.

"Kills Bear with Knife screamed for the Cree warriors to fire their guns. I knew what it meant but probably none of the Snakes did. When the thunder sounded two of them plummeted like grouse from the sky. Their horses took fright and scattered. We shot three warriors with arrows while the guns were reloaded. Then the thunder again. The Snake horses reared in fright, trumpeted, fought the reins, ran. One of them trampled Kills Bear's youngest son where he crouched with an arrow in his thigh. Everything happened so fast. Another of our party had a lance pinning his guts to the prairie.

"That was two of the four we lost in the fight. Then Elk Sky took an arrow in his lung. He would not die until later, on the walk back to camp.

"Another Snake jumped from his horse when the horse was shot. He tried to climb up behind a friend, but Antelope Runner got him first. The Snake dropped with an arrow in his back. He fell, rolling.

"I guess Antelope Runner could not wait to count coup on him. He threw himself over the Snake's body. And the Snake warrior turned with his knife and slew him.

"We buried Antelope Runner in a cairn of stones so that the wolves could not get him. There are no trees in that country, so we could not do a tree burial. We all carried rocks for the cairns. Big cairns.

"We traveled home by following the night stars, because we did not know how many others were at that Snake encampment. No one pursued us. I believe they were frightened of us, because of our guns. Now they know we are mighty.

"Mother, I have told you everything, and I hope you do not wish I had been silent."

Tears ran down Three Catcher's face. She rocked herself in her misery, side to side, while Kit Fox stroked her shoulder. Struggling to stop the tears, she cried, "Now I know Antelope Runner is really dead."

Bad Eyes stammered, "It is better to die in battle than of old age or sickness. Antelope Runner lived bravely." He seemed to realize that no words were of great use, here. With his strong arms, he embraced his mother. "It was a good death. There will not be any more Snake raids. We will buy guns from the Cree and the Cutthroats, we will raid horses from the Snakes. Everyone will fear the mighty Blackfoot!"

Later that day, Kit Fox went down to the lake and cut off her hair. Now everyone who looked at her would know that she, too, was in mourning for Antelope Runner. She felt her heart lift with relief because she had done something to show her sorrow. It was too great to hold inside.

She wandered farther down the shoreline to where it broadened into a flatland meadow, with a wooded bluff at one end where the swallows wheeled over their nests in early summer. The clay cliffs were deserted now. Once their babies left the nests, the swallows fed from new locations. Soon, the first hoarfrost would whiten the grass, and the warm weather birds would all flock south. In this meadow was the horse's pasture. She had not been here for more than a moon's time. And there was Eagle Flies Over Hills, nickering in surprise at her arrival.

A young man sat nearby. His back was to Kit Fox, his head rested on his arms and his arms rested on his knees. For a heartbeat, she hoped it was Found Arrow. Had he at long last returned? The man moved at the sound of her footsteps.

"Come, talk with me," he said. It was Raven Tail Feathers.

Kit Fox walked to Eagle Flies Over Hills and laced her arms around his neck. She pushed her face against the warm, sweaty, dustiness of his hair. But this was too sudden for the horse. He snorted against the strangely short ends of her hair and stepped backward.

"Forgive me," she whispered to him. "I missed you very much." She offered her hands in a firm, slow gesture of appeasement. To Raven she said, shyly, "I forgot how long it has been since he last saw me. Are you on guard duty?"

"Yes," he told her, "until dark."

Kit Fox remembered the old guard warning her not to be seen alone with a man. She did not want to risk gossip, especially with Raven Tail Feathers. Even time near Eagle Flies Over Hills was not worth that. Kit Fox hugged the horse good-bye. He nudged her cheek gently with his nose. How she wished she could ride him again! She wondered if the time would ever come.

Kit Fox smiled and explained to Raven that she must

go. "Many Deer is so glad you returned from the war trail safely. She will be expecting me to help her scrape a moosehide for tanning. I only wandered down to the lake for a moment. I will tell her that I saw you here, that you were on guard duty."

"You chopped off your hair," Raven Tail Feathers said. "I have always thought your hair was one of your greatest beauties. I am sad. But it will grow again."

"The short hair shows my mourning for Antelope Runner. I stopped only because the horse grazes here, and Found Arrow and I always—I must go back to camp now." Suddenly she heard her own voice in her ears, stumbling and stuttering.

Perhaps that was why Found Arrow's brother answered so gently. "You miss him?"

"I—we—enjoy talking and . . ." Kit Fox's voice trailed off.

"Many Deer and I enjoy talking, too. Kit Fox, you would be welcome to share our lodge. I always intended to ask your parents for you, when you became old enough, and that is what Many Deer wants also."

She heard herself say, "I want to have a man with no other wives for my husband," and suddenly she realized how deeply that was true. She knew that very few women chose to have co-wives and most Blackfoot families were one man and one woman. Except, of course, in times of heavy warfare when many men died. Much as Kit Fox loved Many Deer, she wanted to be an only wife. More than that—she wanted a husband who did not seek more than one woman. Now she had said it to Raven Tail Feathers.

"No Blackfoot woman need have a husband she does not want," Raven Tail Feathers replied.

Kit Fox was grateful that that was true. If she could not choose her husband, at least she could refuse any offer of marriage she did not wish.

The washing of the lake against the shore covered the awkward silence. Kit Fox noticed a hoard of mosquitoes landing on the horse. Eagle Flies Over Hills switched at them with his tail but there were places he could not reach. She brushed her palm across his forehead, his chest, his flanks, the sensitive and downy softness of his nose. The mosquitoes scattered.

Now she must steal back to camp.

Kit Fox stared at the lake. Something had jumped in it: splash, splash, splash. Three splashes, close together. Raven Tail Feathers grinned at her startled face.

"I threw three pebbles," he explained. He seemed happier, now that he had surprised her. "You are too much a child for man and woman arrangements. I understand."

"Too young except to watch my elders," she agreed.

"Ask Many Deer. She will tell you all you need to know, and then you will not need to be too young anymore. Does Many Deer work by the tipi with you this afternoon?"

"Yes." Kit Fox stepped deliberately toward the campsite trail. She added, wondering why as she said it, "Many Deer also cut her hair."

Raven Tail Feathers said, "I will comfort her." At her questioning look, he added, "I will be a good husband."

Clouds drifted above them, like puffs of cotton grass. From overhead a sprinkling of rain began to fall. Kit Fox danced on the toes of her moccasins, wanting to run for cover. She managed to make herself say, "I hope you have a long, happy marriage."

She was glad to have said it. And maybe it was possible. More than once he had surprised her. She hoped he would again.

CHAPTER TWELVE

How do you think green triangles would look, with a yellow outline?" asked Kit Fox. Light streamed in through the tipi's open door and across the hide box before her.

Many Deer picked up the parfleche in her hands. "I would prefer green triangles with a red outline. We still have red paint, do we not, from the pussywillows last spring?"

"If you want. The parfleche is a present for you, for your household when you marry." Kit Fox mixed the paint pigments with hot water and glue. Then she ruled in the outline, using peeled willow sticks to mark the straight lines. Even Swift Hands Woman commented on her fine choice of pattern.

When Swift Hands Woman suggested filling in the outline using the porous surface of a rounded bone brush, Kit Fox reached for it. Only Swift Hands Woman knew how to suggest such things, making everything sound as if she was giving nothing but praise. Even better, once her opinion was given she turned away as if she did not care if it was followed.

The old ladies chatted over their cups of mint tea. Raven Tail Feathers' mother was their guest this morning. She had come to borrow their giant copper kettle for a feast.

"But only if you do not need it," she insisted.

"No, that would be fine," Swift Hands Woman assured her.

All three women agreed that their health was fine, the weather fine for the time of year, the mint tea pleasant to the stomach. "You can use the same leaves to flavor pemmican," Raven's mother said.

"Or to line a parfleche of dried meat for the winter," observed Swift Hands Woman.

"Very good, very good," Old Holy Woman agreed, nodding over her tea. After a moment's silence she added, "For painful breathing this type of mint also works wonders—"

Kit Fox clutched her chest behind the old ladies' sight, where only her sister could see her. "Unggh—" she pretended to choke, but quietly. "What ails my breathing?"

"Tell me," whispered Many Deer, stifling giggles.

"I do not know for certain, but I think I am about to die of boredom," teased Kit Fox.

Many Deer held a hand over Kit Fox's mouth. "Baby sister," she asked, without hiding her affection, "do you not think it is time you became serious? Such silliness would not become a wife and mother."

"You are the one who wishes to have children now. I only wish to be free to laugh with my friends."

"You are not going to have children while you are so silly?"

"I want to be silly sometimes. I will have children when I want to work hard almost all day. Soon. Perhaps when I have seen nineteen summers, or twenty. Then I will be a good mother—one who has had enough time first for laughter. Believe me?" With a sweep of her brush, Kit Fox completed her design.

"Ah. A few giggles in private with your husband might not hurt anybody. I believe you. And I like your design," answered Many Deer, her hand patting the side of the parfleche in thanks.

Shoulder against shoulder, they admired it. In the background they heard the clatter of the old ladies' visitor leaving with their kettle.

"We heard you agreeing with Raven Tail Feathers' mother about how good the weather continues," Many Deer informed their grandmother. "Did we understand you to say that the copper trade kettle is good also, and even the horse, and the guns?"

Old Holy Woman laughed her hearty belly laugh. "Nothing could upset me today. Even those things are good."

"The things that come to us from napikwan, they are good?" asked Kit Fox.

"If they are not good, we will make them good—we will control them. How the Blackfoot shall live now, in freedom and strength, on the prairies! Yes, you are right. I was afraid at first of what might come when we went apart from the old ways. Now I think, if we try, we can use these new ways for our purposes."

Swift Hands Woman added, "Some of the new ways need time to learn."

"Like riding the horse?" suggested Kit Fox.

"But we will learn power over them," ended Old Holy Woman, confidently. She put an arm around Kit Fox and drew her closer for a moment.

The co-wives exchanged glances. They are so different, thought Kit Fox. One scrawny and one fat. One short and one even taller than she is round. Yet how they love each other—with thirty-five years of chosen sharing, in the tipi of a husband both had loved and had outlived. As solid as sisters. She decided not to let choices about husbands separate her from her friends or from her affection for Many Deer.

"That napikwan has things to learn from us, too," stated Old Holy Woman. "Perhaps in the end he will have to make some big changes. And why do we do all of this?" She spun on her moccasins. How light she was for such a big woman! She wrapped a plump arm around Cub, just coming in the door, as if she was the whip and he was the spinning-top.

Cub smiled up, puzzled and pleased, into the grin on his grandmother's face. She tickled his stomach. She said, "We do it for this one!"

He squirmed, and butted against his grandmother. She pretended to puff with effort as she let his small weight rock her. Finally she protested, "Aiii, you are already too strong for me!" As Old Holy Woman sank to the floor, Cub snuggled into her arms so she might cradle him. Her wrinkled lips crooned a lullaby.

Swift Hands Woman helped stuff the painting tools

into their kit. "Perhaps you want to lie down early on your sleeping-couch?" she suggested to Many Deer.

"So early?" Many Deer protested.

"Tomorrow you go to your new husband. I was only suggesting you might want to be fresh and beautiful for that." Swift Hands Woman pretended to smirk.

Many Deer dared to smirk in return. "But you should sleep, too. I want you to be fresh and beautiful tomorrow for the exchange of gifts."

"I am so glad to see this." The old lady drew the drawstring of the kit pouch shut, tying it with a flourish. "It is the last new marriage that I shall see."

"Or I," their grandmother raised her face, smiling serenely. "The children are all that is important now."

"Not to us!" cried Many Deer and Kit Fox, almost in unison. Many Deer laid her hand over her sister's wrist, and continued for both of them. "You old women, you are the most important people in the world for us. Who shall we learn from, if we do not learn from you?"

Old Holy Woman laughed at that, holding her stomach so that the shaking would not wake Cub, now asleep. "You forget what we have taught you already. Why do the warriors sing the Going-Away Song? 'We go, but still the women shall bear children, Our tribe shall go on.' Why did Clay Hunter starve himself so that his young sons might have food to live?"

Swift Hands Woman said, "Why do the old ones sing Neetah-hah-yucki when they can no longer follow on the long marches? 'I am many.' Because we live in our children."

Swift Hands Woman with her gnarled finger traced

141

Cub's eyes. Old Holy Woman's head was bent downward, so she could not see her co-wife's face quiver with mischief. "What do you think? Shall I tickle the little one and wake him?" Swift Hands Woman added.

"Sometimes you are still as silly as a girl," admonished Old Holy Woman. Kit Fox thought that her grandmother's voice was shaky with laughter.

"You should remember. Ahh, shall we?" The old ladies attacked the sleeping child with their merciless fingertips. Old Holy Woman demanded, "Where did my extra sack of pemmican go when it disappeared, eh, eh?"

"The dogs—ate—it—" gasped Cub, his cheeks rosy.

Swift Hands Woman said, "You are right, sister, those dogs are bad, starving mutts. I guess we must feed them. And what shall we feed them, now your pemmican is gone?" The old ladies were stumbling toward the door, Cub's struggling body suspended between them.

"You—cannot!" he spluttered.

"No? Why not?"

Cub said, "Because people cannot eat dogs— Sisters, save me!"

Many Deer smoothly said, her hand hiding her laughter, "But how disobedient we would be, not to let our grandmothers do what they want."

"So why can we not?" interrupted Old Holy Woman.

"Because if people cannot eat dogs, dogs cannot eat people!"

Swift Hands Woman asked, "Do you think he is right?"

"No. But I think he is too fat for the dogs." His grandmother bounced her burden into the air.

"It is so," said Swift Hands Woman, patting Cub's

belly sadly. "He might give them indigestion." They dropped him on the floor and Cub joined in their laughter.

The sun at the dawn of that clear day cast its light orange, bright as an oriole's breast. Many Deer washed her hair specially for Raven Tail Feathers, in rainwater colored by meadow rue. Kit Fox assisted by pouring the mixture, while her sister twisted her long locks, so every strand was washed. In her mind she always connected the scent of meadow rue with Many Deer. The older sister often used the herb to soften her hair, and untangle it, and lend a lingering perfume.

With hair still damp, the young women hurried back to their home. They found their mother unpacking the family's good clothes to air on a rack in the sun. Dawn past, the golden light promised warmth by midday. Three Catcher rubbed her arms against the slight chill that lingered.

"How lovely your hair smells," she said as her daughters joined her. Her hand plucked at a quillwork band on their father's shirt which needed restitching. "See this? But at least it can be mended. Much worse is that someone forgot to put the moth repellent stones in the packs for our best clothes."

"Are we lucky? Can any damage be mended?" Many Deer shifted nervously onto one foot.

"Aiii—"

"My dress?" worried Kit Fox. Her mother's face was turned from them. But it was because she was hiding her smile.

"No, no damage. Next time be more careful to include the moth repellent."

"Someone raised those girls to take teasing graciously," Old Holy Woman remarked, as she joined them. "Such delicate smells in the air! Meadow rue and—did some wise person braid sweetgrass to scent our packs of good clothing?"

"I did," Kit Fox admitted. She thought her mother had asked her to also put in chunks of selenite as moth repellent but, if so, she had forgotten.

Together with Many Deer's friends they dressed the wife-to-be in her new gown of soft, white buckskin. "Many Deer, how beautiful you are," breathed Song Sparrow.

"Pray that no rain falls on me today," laughed Many Deer, "or this dress may change back to rawhide."

"It is sad that white buckskin turns in the rain," murmured Song Sparrow.

At midday the main gift arrived from Raven Tail Feathers' parents: a strong travois dog and travois. Whiteweasel and Three Catcher stepped forward together in glad acceptance. By this action they agreed to take the young man for their son-in-law. Everybody already knew they would, and everybody already knew that Many Deer would not say no, either. But still, the ceremony told everyone that the marriage had officially begun.

"Good," approved Three Catcher, examining the red-painted pottery sent on the travois.

"Good. Glad to have it," said Whiteweasel, holding up a hawk-feather fan and flourishing it above his head so all the onlookers might see.

Then they heaped Many Deer's own travois and the travois they now sent as the main present with more gifts for the family of her husband-to-be. They piled on, in turn, a willow backrest, a bag of everyday moccasins, containers of meat, fleecy buffalo robes and—this last drawing a gasp from the spectators—a string of the dentalium shells used by some distant tribes. Many Deer walked by the travois with her own gift of moccasins for Raven Tail Feathers. By his acceptance of the last gift, she would become his wife.

"Do you think that old travois we are sending is fine enough?" whispered Swift Hands Woman to Kit Fox.

The question barely caught Kit Fox's attention. She had been wondering whether to jostle her way to the front of the crowd, so she could see Many Deer arrive at her new tipi. Instead she pressed her arm under the thin and shaky arm of the old lady. Swift Hands Woman herself would of course obey the taboo against looking directly at the new son-in-law. But otherwise, they could watch. At least they need not be left too far behind. The whole camp must be there—dozens of people swarmed between her and Many Deer.

She said, absent-mindedly. "A fine travois."

"Aha! You wish you could see Many Deer from here." Swift Hands Woman was amused. But her chuckle quickly turned to a cough, and her skinny old body leaned with all her weight on Kit Fox. The girl was startled at the whistling breath of the old lady. But Swift Hands Woman insisted, "It is nothing very bad, just the dust. Tell me again. You liked the travois we sent to Raven Tail Feathers' parents?"

Kit Fox struggled to remember details. "A strong travois. Well-built. The best four-pole travois I have seen. How did mother come to have it?"

The old lady managed something of a laugh. At last Kit Fox had said what Swift Hands Woman wanted to hear. "Three Catcher traded a dress I sewed to Kills Bear with Knife's wife. Not a dress worthy of the travois, but fine enough. See?" She tossed her head toward the pretty, older woman who strutted beside Kills Bear.

The dress was indeed lovely. Kit Fox knew how much pride Swift Hands Woman took, and rightly, in the care and extravagance of her special sewing. Kit Fox said, "Four rows of elks' teeth on the chest? Both front and back?"

"Their motion draws the eye as she walks, does it not? She supplied the elks' teeth, of course, but it was my design and my suggestion. Ah, they stop now, we are to the young couple's new tipi. We may catch up with the others. Come—"

The crowds parted for them, so they could see Many Deer's arrival at the tipi. Raven Tail Feathers strode forward to greet the woman who would now be his wife. Even Kit Fox, had she been asked right then, could not have denied his standing as an exceptionally fine-looking man. His piercing eyes, his broad shoulders, his black hair that was tied with swansdown and eagle feathers, and the grizzly bear claws around his neck, that proved his looks were matched by courage. . . .

Many Deer looked up at him, her eyes filled with joy. How glad Kit Fox felt to see Many Deer's happiness that day! How much she hoped her sister would have many happy times from this marriage, more happy times than sad ones.

146

Kit Fox could not wonder at her sister being in love with Raven. Perhaps any woman would be, if she believed she had his love. Even Kit Fox, who knew him so much better, felt her heart stirred by his deep voice as he accepted what Many Deer brought. Their fingers twined for a moment as she placed her gift in his hand.

That is all, then, Kit Fox thought.

Swift Hands Woman said, "It is done. His parents have taken their gifts. He has taken the moccasins. She is his wife now." She leaned heavily on Kit Fox's arm to whisper in her ear, as if confidentially, "I do hope he will be a good husband. When I was a young girl I thought that was the same thing as looking like a hero, do you know?"

Kit Fox hid her sigh. "Yes, I know."

"Good. Now we can all go into the lodge for the feast and more giving of presents. I can imagine the taste of the buffalo berries, as if they were in my mouth already. If only Raven Pinfeathers' mother has the sense to cook them with plenty of grease! She is not always generous, you know. My old nose is dull—can you smell if they are cooking?"

CHAPTER THIRTEEN

Many Deer glowed like a star when their eyes met, Found Arrow—just like in the old stories about lovers. You could have made a song about those two. They looked so happy and so beautiful," Kit Fox told him.

Found Arrow grunted. His face was thin, and she looked for other signs of his long fasting. He was pale and deep, dark circles sat under his eyes. She could not tell if he was listening to her. Yesterday he had returned from his vision quest; this morning they sat on the hillside so at last they might talk together—but his whole attention seemed to be for Cub.

Found Arrow tickled one of Cub's feet as Cub lay on his stomach in the grass. The boy's plump body quivered and he tried to hold back his laughter. Cub managed to hold his outstretched fingers steady though, offering food to the chipmunk perched in front of him.

"Found Arrow?" Kit Fox asked what she most wanted

to know. "Do you think you will be guard again? I want to ride Eagle Flies Over Hills."

"Talk to Kills Bear about him," Found Arrow said as he circled the arch of Cub's foot.

Kit Fox protested, "Stop it. Poor Cub. You are bigger than he is and, anyhow, the ants are helping you."

True. The black biters crawled up one side of the boy, a few stopping to wave a foot or two in the air as they climbed. A miniature war party vanished into the back of Cub's leggings. Cub scratched without looking.

The chipmunk crept to an arrow's length away from Cub's hand. His long, glossy tail twitched. Should he trust Cub or not? The boy was small. And he held food. Or so Kit Fox guessed the chipmunk thought. And she saw the hopefulness on her young brother's face.

"Let Cub be," she hissed at Found Arrow.

She plucked a handful of the luminous white moons of snowberries from the bush to her left, and threw them so they bounced like hail against Found Arrow's shoulder. He ignored her. "Look," she joked, "we have been here so long that already the leaves are turning color. Why do we not walk down toward camp, and let Cub follow?"

Found Arrow gazed around as if surprised. The leaves of the birch shone sunshine yellow, and the green, pointed leaves of the black poplar had yellow borders. The brief northern summer was almost ended.

A sparrow hawk hovered above them in the lazy air, his wings humming like insects. His back shone blue as reflected sky when he dived for an unwary mouse. Kit Fox hoped the mouse could hide under rose thorns, or under the spreading snowberry bushes.

149

She saw that Found Arrow was still tickling her brother. This time Cub let out the beginning of a giggle. His chipmunk started at the sound and leapt back, wary.

"Leave Cub alone," the girl hissed. "He needs to be happy again, to play."

"He is happy when I tease him," Found Arrow insisted.

"He misses Antelope Runner."

"Bad Eyes and I will make up for that."

"He misses having a hero." She hoped her comment had not hurt her friend.

Found Arrow laid the boy's foot down. "There are many kinds of heroes. Maybe what you mean is that Cub needs a hero like Raven Tail Feathers."

Cub's small brown back was rigid now with his concentration on the chipmunk nibbling from his fingers. His sister smiled as she looked at him. To Found Arrow she said, "What I meant was that Cub misses his brother, and your friendship would help him." She held up a hand to shield her burning eyes.

After a pause, Found Arrow asked, "Kit Fox, are you grieving for Antelope Runner?"

"Yes," admitted Kit Fox. Then her grief, too long withheld, spilled out of her. "I miss Many Deer, too. Our family has changed so much. Even our father misses them, Bad Eyes says. He says he never thought our father would notice the marriage of a daughter. But," and suddenly she grimaced, "he notices that Many Deer is gone."

"Your brother gone and your sister married," he observed. "What else is changed?" He cupped Cub's ankle in his hand.

150

"Eagle Flies Over Hills. I never pet him now, feed him treats, ride him. I cannot be seen there. I also miss how you and I talked when we were together, Found Arrow," Kit Fox said.

"Kit Fox . . ."

"Working with Eagle Flies Over Hills was so beautiful," she said. "I have missed laughing with you and all our happy times at the horse meadow. Did you hear me praying, in your visions? I feared Cougar would find you."

"My friend. But Cougar did find me," said Found Arrow. "He gave me much spiritual power."

They smiled at each other.

Cub rolled onto his back. Bits of dried grass stuck to his belly. "Can we go back to camp?" he asked. "Mother said she would boil a kettle of moose meat."

They paused together on the last rise to look down on the lake and the camp. Something was very wrong. No smoke was rising. A dog barked once and then was quiet. Only grown men and women moved between tipis, hurrying without stopping for speech.

Kit Fox felt her senses tingle. Danger. She saw that Found Arrow recognized it also. Cub, impatient from standing still so long, stepped forward, but Kit Fox halted him with a palm laid flat on his head. First they must know the reason for the silent camp.

Two hills away in the direction of the sun, they glimpsed a cloud of brown dust swirling from stampeding wood buffalo. Were these driven by Blood hunters? Why else would they run? But the watchers on the rise heard no distant shrieks, saw no shadows of wolves or coyotes in motion; nothing. Nothing except the dust cloud and

151

its dark core. Next Kit Fox saw a flock of cranes fly over the hills, journeying south. As the shadow of the birds passed over the dust cloud, the girl gasped. The dark forms in the swift-moving cloud were too tall for buffalo.

Just then Found Arrow touched her shoulder and whispered, "Snake people on horseback. I think the scouts must have already seen them. That is why the camp is so quiet."

A revenge party, thought Kit Fox. "What do we do?"

"Run for camp."

"Yes. But are the Cree still here?" Already Kit Fox's mind was racing ahead.

"No, they left earlier this morning. Just before you and I took Cub for a walk." Found Arrow stared at Kit Fox.

"We had better see Cub gets back to camp," she said, staring back.

"Yes." Then Found Arrow paused and finally said, "Kit Fox, there is one way to defeat the Snakes—"

"We need the Cree's guns to fight the raiders."

"They must be almost to the fork of the northern river by now. That is where they left their canoes." Found Arrow's shoulders sagged. "We cannot catch them."

"So close," said Kit Fox. "If Antelope Runner were alive, he could race there and bring them back." She bit around the edge of one finger. "Or maybe not, we will never know." Her voice broke.

Cub tossed his head. He tried to pull away from his sister's grip. "Antelope Runner would have chased them!" he exclaimed. "He would have brought back the weapons that make thunder!"

"Someone from camp has probably gone by now," Found Arrow told him.

"No one else can run fast enough." The little boy looked near crying.

Kit Fox felt her body shake with excitement. She knew what had to be done. "Found Arrow, I could—"

"I could ride Eagle Flies Over Hills," he said.

They stared at each other, the air crackling around them as if lightning might strike at any moment.

"Run home to the tipi, Cub," Kit Fox warned. Then, when he did not move, "Now! Run!"

Found Arrow scooped the child up into his arms. "Put your arms around my neck and I will carry you. But once we reach the horse, Cub, you will have to be ready to run for camp like a deer when the wolves are behind him."

Kit Fox started scrambling down the slope to the horse's meadow. She needed to move. Run or fight, her body demanded. Already her mind was fixed on the Cree path northward. She would not stand helpless to watch the Snakes kill her people. Found Arrow thought he was going to ride the horse for assistance. But she knew otherwise. He was too fatigued and weak from his vision quest. Her path lay clear before her.

They burst through willow and dogwood scrub into the horse's clearing. Raven Tail Feathers turned to face them, his bow in hand, braced, an arrow already notched on the string. Found Arrow yelled a protest. Raven let the bow drop. And Kit Fox saw Sun Smokes standing behind Raven, the horse's bridle in his hand.

She ran, circled Sun Smokes, and grabbed for the bridle.

"No!" Sun Smokes dived away from Kit Fox. "What

are you doing? The Snakes are coming. You must go to the camp!"

Kit Fox said, "I know. We saw. Can you ride, Sun Smokes?"

"No. But—"

"Found Arrow and I can. Let me hold the horse. You do not have to miss the battle. All our band's warriors will be needed at the camp."

Sun Smokes hesitated. Kit Fox guessed how much he must wish to be with the warriors, not to be left with the horse like one too young to fight.

Found Arrow spoke up from where he stood by Raven. "I am going to ride after the Cree traders," he said. "It is true, Sun Smokes. You can join the fight."

Kit Fox lifted the reins from Sun Smokes's hand. Eagle Flies Over Hills snuffled her neck in greeting. Kit Fox knew she was the only one to ride him. Now she must try to convince the men. Every moment lost arguing brought their enemy closer.

The warriors were yelling at each other. "Found Arrow, you are weak from fasting for your vision quest," stated Raven Tail Feathers. "Even if you know how to ride, you cannot ride in this state."

"Weak!" Found Arrow protested, wincing. Cub clung to his leg, wide-eyed and quiet. Found Arrow continued, "You just do not want me to do what you cannot do."

"That is untrue," Raven Tail Feathers glared at Found Arrow. "I am your older brother, hear me—"

"Kit Fox, bring the horse here," said Found Arrow.

Kit Fox swallowed hard. Soon she must say she would ride the horse, herself. For now, she stayed where she was and wrapped her hand in the bridle.

"That is right, Kit Fox," said Raven, "do not give that horse to him."

"Kit Fox!" Found Arrow held out his hand. "Are you my friend?" When she did not move, he strode toward her.

She stepped backward. "Yes," she said. "That is why I tell you that you must not waste yourself in this way. You are needed for the battle, all of you warriors."

They stared at her. "But, Kit Fox," said Found Arrow, "I must ride Eagle Flies Over Hills. Who else can?"

"I can," she said. For the length of a heartbeat no one replied.

"You crazy woman." Raven Tail Feathers' voice broke the silence. "If you do not take the child and run for camp right now, I will—"

"It is you who cannot be spared in camp," she stated. "You, the warrior. And while we are arguing, the Snakes are coming nearer. We all remember the slaughter the last time they attacked the Bloods. Please, you must let me go."

Again she stepped backward, toward the trailhead. The horse neighed as she tugged at him.

"Kit Fox. You are not strong enough." Found Arrow followed her.

"I promise you, though I am no warrior woman, I have a woman's power of endurance," she insisted quietly. "You know I have the strength of the visions sent me by First Maker. Strength to live them. It will be strength enough." She jumped up on the horse. A sense of urgency drove her. "Let me ride for the Cree thunder. I will go. I must go. You must keep our people safe."

Found Arrow grasped the bridle and held her. "But—"

155

Kit Fox tried to speak with the strength of her vision. "Found Arrow, you know I am the one to go. I am the one the beast knows," she said. "You are needed here. You men are the heroes."

From across the meadow, Cub's eyes shone like night stars. "I want to be a hero, too," he announced, staring worshipfully up at the warriors.

The faintest trace of a smile touched Found Arrow's face. "Well, brother," he said, "this woman seems determined to see us be heroes."

He let go of the bridle. Eagle Flies Over Hills whinnied, but calmed under Kit Fox's low chant of praise. She sensed his nervousness, and she stroked his neck with murmurs of reassurance. Kit Fox swung him toward the trailhead, only to find Raven Tail Feathers blocking her path. While she was busy with the horse he had outflanked her.

She felt the powerful muscles of the horse under her legs, ready to run. "Go to the aid of the camp, now," she begged. "There is no more time for the people of our band to fight each other."

Raven Tail Feathers stared at her as if she did not make sense. To Kit Fox's surprise, Sun Smokes now raised his voice. "Let her go," he said. He held out Raven's weapons, and, shaking his head, Raven went over to take them.

Found Arrow motioned Kit Fox to bend down, so he might speak quietly. She leaned close.

"What you have offered is dangerous. You have never ridden a horse so far—none of us have. You are not strong enough. Let me ride," he pleaded.

"My friend, do not worry." Her hands shook as she felt along the horse's neck for his reins.

Found Arrow said, "Earth and sky, hear me: you must not risk your life. Let me risk mine. I—"

She stopped him. "Each of us must do the task we have in our hands. I am going and—and I promise to keep myself as safe as I can. Go. Take your gamble. Let me take mine."

She leaned from the horse, one hand clutching the long mane, to feel Found Arrow's cheek beneath the palm of her hand. How thin he was from his fasting! A great warmth kindled inside her. "Be brave—" she faltered.

"But not heedless," finished Found Arrow, and suddenly he was grinning. It was Kills Bear with Knife's favorite saying.

As Kit Fox leaned forward on the horse's bare back and pressed her knees into his side, she thought, I bet that is how Kills Bear with Knife lived to be an old as well as a famous warrior.

As she wheeled and rode north, she tried to still the beating of her heart so she could think through her course. She knew to follow the north trail—she remembered it well from the year her family had traveled north to make their winter camp at the great fork of the Battle River. Up and down the Eagle Hills the trail ran rough. She would make better time once onto the flatland woods and then the prairie. The last part of her journey, the lush woodland that bordered Battle River, she knew would be slow. Now the sun was blazing almost at midpoint in a clear sky. By the time it started its descent she needed to be all the way to the fork of the river. From the fork the Cree traders always floated their canoes. If Kit Fox did not reach them before they took to the water, her people to died.

She wondered, can I reach the Cree in time? Will I even last the journey? Maybe Found Arrow spoke the truth. Maybe I am not strong enough.

In a sudden rush of courage, Kit Fox promised herself she would not weaken her spirits by thinking of failure. She would think only of victory. She was riding the horse! She was fulfilling her vision. Power flowed through her veins. She knew First Maker rode with her, and First Maker would find a way for her people to be saved.

She traveled without a weapon. On the back of the elk dog, she felt safe. No weapon could help her ward off a group of attackers. She left her safety to the power of the First Maker.

She urged Eagle Flies Over Hills to a trot on the way down the first wooded valley. Kit Fox did not press him, but neither did she let him rest on the slow climb back up.

"Pitiful ponokamita," she whispered, leaning over his neck. She smelled the sweat of his effort. His hair glistened, and she felt his side damp beneath her hand as she stroked him, urging him onward. She dared not permit the rest for which they both panted. "It is a longer ride than I am used to, also. But we must go on. Be brave, my beautiful horse." He neighed in reply, and they galloped on.

She prayed for a view through the stunted trees. She chanted to keep up courage for the horse and herself.

Once out of the hills, the horse shifted his gallop. The girl's body ached with the rhythm, and her ears throbbed. Beat, beat, beat, beat. The hooves now drummed four beats to a stride where before they drummed three. She held tight and balanced with care.

Part of her mind watched for holes ahead of the horse's hooves. Another part strained for sight of the traders. And part longed for any end to her weary hurt. The sun shone past the midpoint of the sky. Her backside was numbed from the continuous motion. Her brain was lulled. She hung carelessly now, letting the horse jolt her along.

As she galloped through the last trees, an overhanging branch slapped out and nearly knocked her down. But she gripped the horse with her thighs, her knees, and her feet. After, she clung to the horse's back and neck with the length of her body. She hung on for the last of the prairie stretch. Her mind flashed to the battle raging at her camp, and still no sign of the Cree.

Thunder boomed from overhead as they entered the river woodlands.

Eagle Flies Over Hills neighed and shied under her. Kit Fox clutched at his neck in panic. She fought to stay on. A sideways buck almost hurled her against the ground, and she cried out. She had a sudden image of herself, neck broken, head shattered under the pounding hooves. No! If she allowed herself to surrender to the animal's fear, then he might throw her. But she did not, this time, have to surrender. Kit Fox concentrated on the strength at her center, as Old Holy Woman had taught her. She cast a robe of peaceful feelings over the horse. For a moment, she thought he would settle.

Suddenly the horse shied again, teeth gnashing, leftward. From behind a tree, Kit Fox watched a hand appear and grasp at the animal's bridle. They swung sideways in a dizzying arc as the horse fought to escape the man. Shades of warriors carrying silver lances spun around them. The horse feinted, shuddering back from the strangers. And stopped.

Eagle Flies Over Hills stood blowing, shivering, his head down, his chest heaving. When Kit Fox looked up, they were surrounded. The heavy-shouldered warrior who held Eagle Flies Over Hills motioned for Kit Fox to climb down from the horse. Now she recognized the man. It was the Cree chief.

Kit Fox slid, legs weak as an infant's, to the ground. The Cree chief shook his head at her. In his other hand he held what she had at first taken for a lance—a gleaming silver musket.

Despite the dizzy black buzzing threatening to engulf her head, and the rising acid in her throat, she smiled at the sight. Her task was done. She had reached them. Now all she had to do was find the right words for her request. If the Cree wished to sell guns to the Blackfoot tribes, they would give what she now asked. My people shall have horses and guns, she thought. I hope they make us mighty.

CHAPTER FOURTEEN

The Cree huddled together for a moment's talk, then set off down the trail on which Kit Fox had just come. She watched until the gleam of the last gun vanished from sight. Then she threw herself down on her back in the long grass and tried to relax the pain in her legs.

Eagle Flies Over Hills rolled an eye at her.

"Rest, my friend," she said. "We must follow them soon."

Every muscle in her body ached. She wanted to lie on her back against the warmth of the earth, her eyes shut, her body soaked in comforting sunlight. But she knew she must follow the Cree.

Even though there was nothing more she could do to change what would happen.

Nothing except pray. Every step of her trail back she prayed to First Maker; she asked for the Cougar's help. Help my people live, she prayed. May the guns not reach them too late.

161

Kit Fox forced herself to keep putting one foot ahead of the other, and forced the exhausted horse, too, hauling on his lead whenever he halted. By the time they reached the Eagle Hills, her strength was almost gone.

By now the sun had slipped a third of the way down its path through the sky. At the crest of every hill the girl had to rest longer. Finally, she saw in the distance the glint of the lake. She flung her arm over the horse's neck.

"Almost there," she promised him. How she wished she was not too sore to ride!

Soon the thunder of the guns sounded in her ears. Kit Fox wondered how she was to get near the camp safely. From the last rise before the horse meadow, she could see puffs of smoke. For a moment she wondered—burning tipis? She bit her lip and ignored the taste of blood.

But no. Not a burning camp. The smoke rose in many small puffs. It was the smoke of guns!

The thunder and smoke came from the southwest side of the camp. So, thought Kit Fox, the Cree arrived while our warriors still held their ground. The children will be safe. She prayed for the men of her family, even for Raven Tail Feathers, and for her friend Found Arrow, also. When she approached the hill above the camp, she counted the bodies of one horse and five warriors upon the ground. From their hair or clothes, she guessed at least four of the warriors to be Snakes. Kit Fox leaned against Eagle Flies Over Hills and watched with clenched fists. She knew she could not help further. Then another Snake tumbled from his mount. Their chief raised his arm to signal to his dozen warriors remaining. Moments later the Snakes turned their horses to flee. Kit Fox yelled in triumph. Gratitude to First Maker for the strength of the vision he had sent almost overwhelmed her.

It was over. It was over.

She started down the slope on legs trembling from weariness. The horse followed.

Eagle Flies Over Hills pawed the feathery snow. A hole grew in the drift; soon stems of weasel grass appeared, plump and whole. He nickered in satisfaction.

"Dee, dee," chirped a bird from overhead.

"The horses and chickadees like this weather," Bad Eyes commented, as they watched the horse their father had bought from the war chief. He warmed his nose with his right hand, the hand that was missing two fingers since the Snake attack of last summer.

Kit Fox searched the barren branches in the direction of her older brother's gaze. Above them the sun gleamed pale yellow, as if frozen behind layers of ice in the early morning sky. There. The chickadee's feathers were fluffed against the frost, yet he looked and sounded quite content with winter.

She returned her brother's grin. She knew Bad Eyes appreciated that without her effort they might not have won against the Snake people.

"Kit Fox, there is something I want to tell you."

"Yes, brother."

"You were very brave," he told her. "We might not have won, if you had not ridden the horse—and known how to ride."

Kit Fox nodded. What he said was no less than the truth. And no greater praise could be given a Blackfoot woman. She lifted his good hand in both of her own and squeezed it. "You were brave, too."

Kit Fox enjoyed the comradeship that had sprung up between them since her ride for the Cree and the guns.

"Now," she teased, "you could say that the horses and chickadees like winter just as much as we do."

"You mean, we have no choice and we can probably survive," he returned.

"And it has its cheerful moments," Kit Fox said.

"Yes. With delicacies like frozen weasel grass."

"There will be fine hunting when we get to the winter camp. How glad I am we take the trail today! It was our bad luck that the snow came early and caught us by surprise," said Kit Fox.

The horse nuzzled into the cold white powder. Kit Fox stepped forward to see better. She exclaimed, "Bad Eyes—he is eating the snow!"

"So he is," agreed Bad Eyes. "Good. He is a tough one. Though I suppose if we had to we could melt snow into water for him. If the snow gets to be too deep we may have to find him some food. Does Eagle Flies Over Hills eat moose meat?"

Kit Fox shivered and slapped her new mittens together, enjoying the solid thud they made. "No, not meat. And I am not going to dig around in the snow to find grass. Perhaps poplar twigs or bark? That is what the deer eat when the snow covers everything else."

Bad Eyes laughed at his sister. "If the horse is wise, he will decide that almost anything we offer is better than starvation. Though there have been times stalking deer in the winter when I was so cold I was not sure my arms could still draw the bow, and I thought warmth was even more important than eating."

She stamped her feet against the cold. "If we do not move soon, my toes will turn to ice."

"I think Mother wants you to help her load the travois," said Bad Eyes. Three Catcher had just left the tipi and was flapping her arms up and down to warm herself.

When Kit Fox came up to her, she handed her daughter the reins to one of the camp's new horses. This one was a pregnant mare, her big black belly easily noticed against the whiteness of the snow. "Raven Tail Feathers loaned her to your father," she explained to Kit Fox. "Do you think you can tie a saddle on her somehow?"

Mother is still a little uneasy with horses, thought Kit Fox, but I do not mind. It gives me something more I can do for her. Her hands reached for the lead.

"Mother! Look at her eyes!" Each of the horse's brown eyes was rimmed with frozen tears.

"She will not be so cold when the band starts moving," Three Catcher answered, her voice dry with practicality. "Many Deer has made large carrying bags to hang from her back and hold supplies. But first she will need you to fasten her saddle."

"I had an important question to ask Old Holy Woman before we left."

"She will be out soon. Better saddle the horse while you are waiting."

The wind whined through the trees, and dusted their ankles with soft snow. As she adjusted the saddle and panniers, Kit Fox admired each piece of her sister's handiwork on these newest items of horse gear. The many-colored quillwork shone brightly against the white of the snowdrifts. Soon Cub ran up to watch, the tipi pegs held tight in one of his hands. When their older sister arrived he greeted her by squealing, "Many Deer!"

Many Deer was dressed for warmth, with one tip of her robe pulled over her head and the tail of it falling to her ankles.

"Is your tipi loaded?" Kit Fox asked. "Can you help here? Would you carry our youngest brother on his cradleboard for this morning's journey?"

Another gust of wind whined through the camp. "Yes. But, Kit Fox," her sister reproached her, "I thought you said this winter would be a mild one."

"I said the blue grama grass had only one spike for each tassel. Old Holy Woman told me that usually means a mild winter. Did I forget to tell you 'usually'? I am sorry."

"Ha!" interrupted Cub. He was trying to climb the horse's tail.

Kit Fox straightened from her task and turned to him. "I dare you to say that again."

The old ladies joined them just as Kit Fox was reaching for her brother. Old Holy Woman grinned and stopped her. "Children, children. Do not fight over predictions. No one can see all of tomorrow. But neither should you fault your sister for trying to foresee what she can. Is it not so, Swift Hands Woman?"

Her fragile co-wife leaned against her, encircled by her arm—good protection, thought Kit Fox, against the cold. They all worked together to hoist Swift Hands

Woman onto the mare. Old Holy Woman handed up the firehorn for her co-wife to carry. With the firehorn went much responsibility, since it carried the coals that would light all the band's later fires.

Now the band chief ordered them to move out. The trek to the winter campsite had begun. This time Kit Fox would lead Swift Hand Woman's mare in the middle of the procession. The girl's whole body radiated happiness. Old Holy Woman had just offered to teach her all of the simplest of the healing arts, the use of the medicine herbs.

"I do not think it is only good and power that comes to us with napikwan's guns," her grandmother had said. "I think our tribe will need more healers. You have followed your vision with great strength. Now I shall teach you many mysteries."

The words kept Kit Fox warm as they slogged through the unending snow, and the sun climbed in the sky. Before it hit midpoint, a warrior joined her. Kit Fox admired how his long, smoky-black hair blew in the wind. She thought, with the eagle feathers tied in his hair, he looks wild enough to fly. It was not very practical, but she was glad to see Found Arrow enjoying himself. She admitted to herself that she liked the way he looked.

Another ornament of feathers dangled from his fingers. With a start, she realized Found Arrow was offering something to her.

"Glad to have it," she said, her eyes wide with wonder. "What is it?"

His voice was so soft that she had to step close to catch the words.

"It is an ornament of golden eagle feathers," he said.

"With a quillwork band. I asked my mother to make it for you. She says you are to tie it in the tail of your horse, so when you ride he may fly like the wind."

Kit Fox bit her lip. What did it mean? She had not thought of marriage yet, not with Found Arrow, not with anyone. And this gift was not one of the ones traditionally sent as a marriage offer. It must mean he had asked for his parents' approval of her. And it must mean they had agreed she would be a good choice. Kit Fox felt an inner glow of warmth, as if she sheltered something that could light many years of hearth fires. She could think of no one finer to share life with than Found Arrow. When she wanted to marry, she would want him.

"Take this as a gift," he said, again holding out the feathers.

"You are generous." Their hands touched as she took the ornament. "I wish I had a horse of my own."

"Then I will have to steal one for you." Found Arrow's face relaxed. "Those are good horses we took from the Snakes, yes? Especially the war chief's pinto pony, and this mare of Raven's."

He reached past Kit Fox to run a hand along the mare's black nose with its blaze of lightning. If ever he had been unfamiliar enough with horses to be shy of them, Found Arrow was not shy now. Kit Fox joined him. Together they stroked the horse.

Found Arrow laughed out loud. "Yes, the Snakes, who have taken so much from us—"

"So many lives, so many wounds. Raven tells me the lump still aches where that Snake club smashed his collarbone. But from them we got our horses." Kit Fox nodded her head. "Still, I prefer Eagle Flies Over Hills to any other horse, anywhere."

She could see her father on Eagle Flies Over Hills, just ahead, as she and Found Arrow fell behind. It was funny to watch the tiny figure of Swift Hands Woman following him on the black mare. Kit Fox knew that, without the horses, the band might have had no choice if Swift Hands Woman insisted she be left behind. But because of the mare she was able to travel in comfort. By the approving comments of friends who came to speak with the old lady, and by their admiring looks, Kit Fox knew horses were now an accepted part of the life of her band.

Found Arrow caught the direction of her eyes, and grinned again. "We will have many more horses soon. We can raid Snake horses, or even farther south, as far as the black-robed napikwan. Or, if we and the Snakes ever make peace—"

"As we have before and will again—"

"They are not bad people when we are at peace with them—then we can trade for their horses."

"Maybe trade horses for guns?" Kit Fox dared to wonder. She and Found Arrow walked with shoulders brushing as they learned to keep time with their steps. She thought, how easy it is to walk with him, and tell him what I hope and feel.

Found Arrow agreed with her suggestion. "Why not trade horses for guns? The Bloods will have many of both before most of the tribes around us do."

"Good times for us. Good times for all the Blackfoot tribes."

He laughed again, confident now and unhurried.

"Good times for our people. And for you and me. Someday we will own many horses, and be able to invite all our friends to our tipi to feast with us and our children. But you are only sixteen, and I am only eighteen. We have time enough to wait."

Kit Fox smiled as she met Found Arrow's eyes. His words were the thought of her heart, also. It was good.

BIBLIOGRAPHY

Arthur, George W., *An Introduction to the Ecology of Early Historic Communal Bison Hunting Among the Northern Plains Indians*, National Museums of Canada, Ottawa, 1975.

Brink, Jack, *Dog Days in Southern Alberta*, Archaeological Survey of Alberta, Occasional Paper No. 28, 1986.

Bullchild, Percy, *The Sun Came Down*, Harper & Row, San Francisco, 1985.

Chittenden, Hiram Martin, *The American Fur Trade of the Far West*, University of Nebraska Press, Lincoln and London, 1986 (reprint).

Corbett, E. A., *Blackfoot Trails*, Macmillan, Toronto, 1934.

Costello, David, *The Prairie World*, University of Minnesota Press, Minneapolis, 1980.

David Thompson's Narrative of His Explorations in Western America 1784–1812, J.B. Tyrell, Toronto, 1916.

171

Dempsey, Hugh A., *Blackfoot Ghost Dance*, Glenbow Foundation, Calgary, Occasional Paper No. 3, 1968.

Dugan, Kathleen Margaret, *The Vision Quest of the Plains Indians: Its Spiritual Significance*, The Edwin Mellen Press, Lewiston/Queenston, 1985.

Ewers, John C., *Blackfeet Crafts*, United States Department of the Interior, 1945.

————, *The Blackfeet: Raiders of the Northwestern Plains*, University of Oklahoma Press, Norman, 1958.

————, "A Blood Indian's Conception of Tribal Life in Dog Days" [a recorded oral history], *The Blue Jay*, 18:44–48 (March 1960).

Highwater, Jamake, *Ritual of the Wind*, Alfred van der Marck, New York, 1984.

Hungry Wolf, Adolf and Beverly (compilers), *Blackfoot Craftworker's Book*, Good Medicine Books, Skookumchuck, BC, 1983.

Hungry Wolf, Beverly, *The Ways of My Grandmothers*. William Morrow & Company, Inc., New York, 1980.

Johnston, Alex, *Plants and the Blackfoot*, Lethbridge Historical Society, Alberta, Occasional Paper No. 15, 1987.

Kehoe, Alice B., "Old Woman Had Great Power," *The Western Canadian Journal of Anthropology*, Vol. VI, No. 3, 1976.

Lancaster, Richard, *Piegan*, Doubleday & Co., Garden City, NY, 1966.

Lewis, Oscar, *The Effects of White Contact Upon Blackfoot Culture: with Special Reference to the Role of the Fur*

Trade, American Ethnological Society Monograph No. VI, J.J. Augusta, Publisher, New York, 1942.

Linderman, Frank Bird, *Blackfeet Indians*, folio, 1935.

McHugh, Tom, *The Time of the Buffalo*, University of Nebraska Press, Lincoln and London, 1972.

Mountain Horse, Mike, *My People, the Bloods*, Glenbow-Alberta Institute and Blood Tribal Council (Standoff), 1979.

Nelson, J.G., *Man's Impact on the Western Canadian Landscape*, Carleton Library, 1976.

Point, Nicholas, S.J., *Wilderness Kingdom: Indian Life in the Rocky Mountains 1840–1847*, Holt, Rinehart & Winston, New York, 1967.

Ray, Arthur J., *Indians in the Fur Trade: Their Role as Trappers, Hunters, and Middlemen in the Lands Southwest of Hudson Bay 1660–1870*, University of Toronto Press, 1970.

Reeves, B.O.K., "Six Milleniums of Buffalo Kills," *Scientific American*, Vol. 249 (Oct. 1983) pp. 120–135.

Schultz, James Willard, *Blackfeet and Buffalo*, University of Oklahoma Press, Norman, 1962.

———, *Why Gone Those Times? Blackfoot Tales*, University of Oklahoma Press, Norman, 1974.

Scrivner, Bob, *No More Buffalo*, The Lowell Press, Kansas City, 1982.

Vickers, J. Roderick, *Alberta Plains Prehistory: A Review*, Archaeological Survey of Alberta, Occasional Paper No. 27, 1986.

Wyman, Walker D., *The Wild Horse of the West*, Caxton Printers, Caldwell, Idaho, 1945.

Jan Hudson first began to think about writing when she became interested in the history of the Blackfoot people after the adoption of her daughter, Cindy Lynn, who is of Blackfoot descent. Her first book, *Sweetgrass*, was named an ALA Notable Book and an ALA Best Book for Young Adults, as well as a Canadian Library Association Book of the Year for Children. It was also the recipient of the Canada Council Children's Literature Prize. *Sweetgrass* has been published in nine countries.

Ms. Hudson lived in Alberta, Canada, until her death in 1990.